Angel in Chains

A Hellfire Novella Book Two

Hayley Briana

<u>DON'T BE A DICK WHO STEALS FROM AUTHORS!</u>

This novel is entirely a work of fiction. The names, characters, and incidents portrayed in it are the work of the author's imagination. Any resemblance to actual persons, living or dead, events or localities is entirely coincidental.

Hayley Briana asserts the moral right to be identified as the author of this work.

First Edition

ISBN: 979-8-9874871-5-0

Cover Art by Hayley Briana
Formating by Hayley Briana

<u>YOU CAN</u>
<u>REPORT PIRATING</u>

Not many people are aware, but if you notice
pirating of an author's work (or any pirating in general)
you can report it anonymously to the FBI.
As we have seen, they can take down a site for pirating.

Supporting these institutions makes you a thief.
NO ONE IS ENTITLED TO SOMEONE ELSE'S
WORK! Pirating is a crime and you can face large fines of
up to $250,000 USD and jail time of 5 years.

If you can't afford the book(s) maybe try reaching out
to the author directly. Many are willing to offer you a free
download of their book.
Also, joining an author's newsletter is a great way to
stay up to date on any sales or freebies they have offered.

**To report pirating you can contact your local
FBI Office and/or report online at
https://www.ic3.gov/ or https://tips.fbi.gov/**

If your panties aren't soaked when you get to that one specific scene, then I've failed at my goal. Happy reading kinky baddies!

CONTENT WARNING

Disclaimer: This book contains explicit content and dark themes that may be considered traumatic and offensive to some readers.
Please check triggers before reading.
If you are uncomfortable with some of these topics please put this book down and do not read it.
This work of adult fiction is only for those 18 or older.

For a complete list of triggers
please visit HayleyBrianaWrites.com

Scan to see a list of triggers

Playlist

Dark Nights - Dorothy

The Death of Peace of Mind - Bad Omens

Shackles - Steven Rodriguez

Harder to Breathe - Letdown.

Punching Bag - Palaye Royale

Dismantled - Icon For Hire

Rewired - Gabbie Hanna

Venom - Icon For Hire

Here Come the Wolves - Lola Blanc

Victim - Halflives

Paralyze - Haunter

Love is a Weapon -Letdown.

Table of Contents

PROLOGUE

It's dark and cold. The air is filled with the scent of damp mold. I can't see anything in front of me through the darkness in the stone room I'm in. A constant drip of water can be heard, and it grates my nerves, leaving me feeling anxious.

I could still feel their hands on me as they dragged me into the van. The drugs they'd used to knock me out had me feeling dizzy and tired as I tried to take in my surroundings. There were no windows, which led me to believe it was a basement of some kind. The constant drip was doing little to help with my pounding headache.

A door cracked open to illuminate the dark space as a darkened figure stood in the doorway.

Someone, please get me out of here.

CHAPTER ONE

Angel

"It's a good plan and I don't need your fucking permission."

Damon stood in front of me, bitching about my plan to get Cherry back. Dimitri was no fucking help, that was for sure. He sat there on the plush couch, looking completely broken. He nursed a tumbler filled with whatever he could get his hands on and there was a good amount of stubble on his usually clean-shaven face. I didn't think he'd ever let himself go like this, but I also couldn't blame him, given the situation.

"It's a shit plan. You'll be on your own."

Damon growled, towering over me.

His sweet mahogany scent wrapped around me, making me feel needy and suffocated at the same time. It had been far too long since I'd been laid and tensions were high at the moment. I wasn't an idiot and wouldn't let myself fall back into bed with the asshole this time around. I barely got out last time and I was positive I couldn't do it again.

"It's a good plan, Damon. She could get in easily and make sure Cherry was safe. If we can track her, we will know exactly where she is and we can make a plan to get them both out." Zack said.

Damon just growled, shooting a glare at his friend. He was really going to get on my fucking nerves. I'd been gone for months and now he wanted to be this overprotective asshole when we had other things to worry about. We needed Dimitri to snap the fuck out of it, and we needed to get everything prepared so that we could get Cherry back.

Walking over to Dimitri, I snatched the drink from his hands and downed what was left in the glass. He glared up at me from his seat and I got directly into his face. "I get it. This is a shit situation, but pouting like a fucking child isn't helping her. Man, the fuck up."

His bloodshot eyes continued to glare at me. "Do whatever you have to do to get her back. You'll have access to all our money and resources."

His words were slurred as he got up from the couch and stumbled out of the room. With one last glare at me, Damon walked out after his brother. Leaving just Zack and me in the lounge. Zack was the only one who was keeping a level head, mostly. I knew he was falling apart, but he was focused on us getting his sister back. His focus would come in handy for getting things prepared. We couldn't afford for everyone to lose their shit.

"I'm going to need the contacts of the people who can help us," I said, collapsing on the couch next to him.

"I'll get them for you, sweetness." He said without looking at me.

I placed my hand on his knee, giving him a comforting pat. "I'm going to get her back, Zack. They fucked with the wrong people."

We spent the rest of the night going over everything that needed to be done, Damon only returning as we finished up for the night. He gave Zack a pat on the back as he walked past, shutting the door behind him. I did my best not to look at the man who'd been the star of my best dreams these past months, as he moved further into the room. Nursing my tumbler as I watched the people down below on the floor of Hellfire. It had been so long since I'd worked those very floors. Almost a lifetime ago. I'd run off as soon as Madax was dealt with and I'd had no intention of ever coming back to this life. There were too many skeletons in the closet. Too much bad blood to build a decent life here. I had needed to find my own place in the world, no matter what I was leaving behind to deal with in the aftermath.

Damon sighed as he took a seat next to me on the sofa, taking the tumbler from my hand to place on the coffee table. "I was still drinking that."

"We need to talk." Damon's gruff voice sounded exhausted before his hand found its way around my throat, forcing me to look at him directly.

A part of me wanted to slit his throat, and yet another wanted him to take me right here. "Get the fuck off me."

My voice dripped with venom and heat as I glared up into his blue eyes, letting my eyes trail down the length of his face. He'd trimmed his beard since I'd seen him last, but it was still long, surrounding his full lips that I knew could bring me immense pleasure. Yeah, it had definitely been too long since I'd been fucked. Now that I think about it, Damon was the last time.

A wicked smirk lit up Damon's face as his hand tightened around my throat. "Play nice, Angel, and I'll let you come."

My heart raced in my chest as I pulled the knife from my boot, holding it to his throat. The feeling of déjà vu washed over me. He always liked to play these sorts of games. Damon's other hand wrapped around my wrist until I was forced to drop my blade. He pushed me by my throat, forcing me onto my back where he hovered over me and I wasn't able to reach him or my weapon.

"That's not nice, Angel." His voice morphed into a deep growl in his chest, and heat pulled at my core from the sound alone.

I moved to scratch my nails down the forearm, keeping me pinned until something cold brushed up my inner thigh, right next to the crudely carved D. This man had branded me the last time I'd been in a similar situation like this. Looking down, my blade was held in his large hand, blood already dripping from his palm as he trailed the hilt under the hem of my skirt.

"What the fuck do you think you're doing?" I forced every ounce of hate I possessed into my voice, bucking and clawing to free myself. Nothing made him budge as the hilt found my entrance. Why had I not worn anything underneath this skirt tonight? The cold metal moved up at an agonizing pace to the bundle of nerves at the apex of my thighs, stimulating until I was panting and my fight dissolved. It was so hard to fight Damon when I was trying not to show him the effect he had on me.

CHAPTER TWO

Damon

It had been too long. Regardless of what we were facing, I needed to bury myself in her cunt. Angel had always had a way of getting under my skin. Every part of me wanted to feel her underneath me. For her scent to surround me as I brought us both to release. She'd pissed me off earlier, and I wanted to take that anger out on her like my own personal toy.

Now that she was beneath me, panting, her thighs spread while I worked her clit with the cold metal of her knife. My hand flared in pain where I gripped the blade, but it only fueled my need to fill her. So much hatred shone in her cold, blue eyes and I took my time to play with her, to admire my little Angel. More tattoos decorated her skin since I'd last seen her. A piece peaking out from between her breast that I wanted to see the extent of what covered her below her sweater. A rose peaked out of the collar, taking up the entire right side of her slender neck. My cock ached, pushing against my zipper as I took her in.

Without warning, I slammed the hilt of the knife into her dripping wet cunt, tearing a moan from her ruby-red lips. Her head tossed back onto the couch as I fucked her with her own knife. I smiled to myself as she came around the knife; her release mixing with my blood that now covered her thighs. Pulling the knife free, I finally tossed it onto the coffee table and let go of her throat. Watching her chest rise and fall as she tried to catch her breath.

I didn't expect my Angel to want me. Not after she'd run off the last time, avenging her dead sister. I was pleasantly surprised when she lashed out, gripping me by my jacket to pull me into a heated kiss. There was never anything soft about this woman.

She took what she wanted and had no intention of caring about anyone else. My hands tangled in her long black hair as she straddled me, her skirt bunched around her hips as she ground against my length, soaking my jeans in the process.

Angel reached between our bodies, working quickly to free my cock, her hands working the length as she positioned herself above me. Our mouths and tongues fought for dominance while she slid down my cock, her warm cunt strangling me as she slid down to the base, forcing me as deep as possible into her heat.

I groaned against her lips, my hands finding her hips as she began to ride me. "That's a good girl. Let that perfect cunt strangle my cock."

She bit at my lip, thrusting her hips faster and I fucked up into her core. Using my hands to slam her down on my cock until I could feel my balls tightening. At this rate, I wasn't going to last long for my little Angel. That wouldn't do. Without missing a beat, I pushed her back onto the floor, thrusting my cock back into her at a punishing speed. Her body arched into mine as her legs wrapped around my waist and she met my thrusts with her own.

Wrapping a hand around her throat, forcing her to look at me and cutting off her air supply, "Come for me, Angel."

At my command, I felt her cunt tighten around me and a flood of heat coat my thighs. I loved how responsive she was to me. Spurring my hips faster until I was coming deep inside her. Holding her there, wishing my hands were enough to keep her here with me this time. I tried not to think of that as I pulled myself from her, flipping her over onto her hands and knees with her beautiful ass up in the air. From this angle I could see the D I'd carved into her creamy thigh, letting my finger lazily trace the crude scar. I wasn't going to let her get away this time, and I was far from done with her.

A rumbling growl left my lips as I sank into her again. "Mine."

CHAPTER THREE

Angel

I was sitting in a makeshift doctor's office in some warehouse off the docks. Of course, the Ashfords had their own personal doctor along with a long list of contacts who could help me get what I needed.

Zack had reached out to their tech guy, Jensen, who created a tracker, and *The Doctor* was going to implant it so that the boys could track me when I went into the lion's den, so to speak. Doc was an older gentleman who appeared to be in his early seventies as he prepped my neck for the implant. I'd made sure it would go on my left side. I didn't need a big ass scar on my new ink.

Wrinkles decorated his face, framing his chocolate brown eyes, and he had very little grey hair at this point. I watched as he meticulously got the needle contraption set up for the implant. It reminded me of those things they used to microchip dogs, but I guess that could be exactly what it was. I'm sure this guy wasn't an actual doctor, considering we were in a warehouse.

"This is going to sting a bit," He said in his aged, wispy voice as he pinched the skin on my neck.

"I'm not scared of a bit of pain, Doc." He hadn't offered me his name when I'd arrived and I wasn't in the mood to ask.

He plunged the oversized needle into my neck, causing me to flinch before he pulled the trigger. Nothing else was said as he slapped a bandage over the wound and sent me on my way. I hope he was good at what he did because he had shit bedside manner.

I made my way out of the warehouse into the salty air. I missed the smell of the water here. This place had been home before everything went to shit.

If I closed my eyes for a second, I could pretend that all the awful shit hadn't happened. I'd had no intention of ever coming back to this shit hole, but I had to admit a part of me belonged here.

A horn honked in the distance, drawing my attention to my old Impala. It looked as if she'd been done up since the last time I'd seen her. I knew leaving the beautiful machine with Damon had been the right thing to do. He'd cleaned up my old car and had her fully restored. The black paint was shiny, and the only thing that gave away the fact that it had been mine at all was the chrome snake mascot on the front hood.

I walked over, running my hand along the hood as I passed, before slipping into the car and sinking into the worn leather seats. I closed my eyes and leaned my head back on the seat as Damon drove off.

"I couldn't bring myself to change your car," Damon said in that deep voice I'd dreamed so many months about. It was rough and sent shivers over my skin in the most delectable way.

"It's not mine anymore." I simply wasn't in the mood to argue, and the rest of the drive was silent.

He said he'd made arrangements for my stay while I was here. I didn't plan on staying once we got Cherry back and we could settle this crap with Madax's old partners, but I felt responsible in a way because I just took him out and ran away. I didn't stick around to see what the aftermath would be or and now my friend had been taken. That twisted my gut. She was a sweet girl who didn't deserve what had happened, and I felt responsible. Just one more person I cared about that I'd failed to protect. I'd do whatever it took to get her back.

We pulled up to my old apartment building, and I glanced over as Damon cut the engine and got out. Why would he bring me here? I was positive he would have sold off my old place.

He didn't even look back to make sure I was following him as he entered the building. I got out of the car and followed him inside as he was making his way up the stairwell. Sure enough, he was opening the door to my old apartment when I made it to the top of the stairs. He left the door open and leaned against the doorframe as I made my way over to him. Stepping inside, I felt a rush of déjà vu. That feeling seemed to be a constant since coming back to my old life here. Nothing had been moved. It was exactly as I'd left it when I wanted out months ago. It had obviously been cleaned, but nothing was out of place. I walked over to my nightstand and found the book I'd started still laying face down to save the page I'd been on.

I heard the booted footsteps and the door shutting as Damon made his way inside while I was looking over everything. I made my way into the small kitchen area and opened the fridge to see that it had been freshly stocked. Including a selection of my favorite drinks. I pulled out two beers and popped the tops off on the counter as I walked over to Damon, offering him a drink. He took it without saying a word, lifting the bottle to his lips. Watching his arms flex and the way his throat bobbed as he took a swig shouldn't have been as sexy as it was. Standing this close to him, all I could smell was his manly scent, and I felt the need to clench my thighs together.

To distract myself, I turned to look around the small space once more while taking a swig of my beer. "You didn't change anything."

"I knew you'd come back eventually," was all he said as he made his way over to my small couch, where he took a seat and propped his booted heels on the scuffed-up coffee table.

I rolled my eyes before taking a seat next to him, leaving a bit of space between us. Things had been so awkward with us since I'd gotten back. The heat was still there, but it was as if something that needed to be said was just hanging in the air around us.

"I didn't plan on coming back, you know," I said before taking another drink.

My drink was yanked from my hand, sat on the coffee table, and I was pinned to the couch before my brain could even process what had just happened. Damon's massive body hovered over me and he gripped my wrists in a tight grip above my head. The anger on his face was apparent as he forced himself between my legs and I bucked, trying to get him off.

"Either you were coming back on your own or I would make the choice for you."

I spit in his face. "You don't fucking own me, Damon."

He growled, using his free hand to wipe the spit from his face. "We will see about that."

Reaching down, he ripped at my jeans, forcing them down my legs as much as he could while I fought to get him off of me. He lifted just enough to flip me onto my stomach before pinning me down with his body. I heard his zipper as he undid his pants before he pulled my hips up to position himself at my entrance.

"Don't you fucking dare!" I screamed, thrashing even harder to free myself from his grasp.

He didn't give a shit and thrust into me. His massive size seemed to tear me in half as he thrust into me. Fuck.. A moan slipped from my lips as he pounded away, forcing his cock deep into my soaking cunt. I'd forgotten how good it felt for him to fill and stretch me to my limits. It didn't matter what my head wanted, my body had other plans. Bending to his will. I thrust my hips back to meet his as the pleasure in my core built. All that I could focus on was the sounds of flesh meeting flesh in rapid succession and our moans of pleasure filling the small room. I was so fucking close already.

He released my wrists and moved his hand to wrap around my throat from behind, cutting off my airway as he pulled me up so that my back was pressed firmly to his hard body.

His lips grazed my ear, the scruff of his beard moving along my skin as he whispered, "Come for me like a good little slut, Angel."

A shiver racked my body as he tightened his grip on my throat until I couldn't breathe and I fell over the edge. My orgasm ripped through me so hard that my vision blackened around the edges. He fucked me ruthlessly through the waves of pleasure that assaulted me until he was roaring out his own release. His cock pulsed inside of me, forcing my eyes to roll back.

He stayed inside of me, propped up on his elbows on either side of me as we lay there, catching our breath. He lightly kissed my shoulder and neck, forcing a breathy moan to escape my lips.

"You're mine, Angel, whether you like it or not." He whispers against my skin before getting up.

He left me lying there, a mixture of emotions filtering through my mind, as he redid his pants. From my position on the coach, I simply watched as he tossed an envelope on the kitchen counter. "From Jensen, he said it's to give him access to the mainframe once you're in."

He didn't look back at me or say another word as he walked out of the apartment, closing the door behind him. All I could do was lay there in a mix of pleasured bliss while my mind raced.

What the hell had I gotten myself into?

CHAPTER FOUR

Angel

I'd started my old job at Hellfire again while we

worked out all the details of the plan. The plan was a

simple one. Make myself available to be snatched up.

Since Dimitri had cut ties with the skin trade, there

had been some backlash and girls kept going missing

from the club. These guys wanted revenge against

Dimitri and Damon. They wanted to cause them pain,

so what better way than to snatch up their girls?

They'd already tried it before, so it should be easy to

do now. I'd even stopped wearing my knife since I

didn't need to be killing these guys before they could

take me to where Cherry was.

It had been about a week of Damon showing

me off as his and working at the club again. I had to

admit I'd missed him while I was away, but I wasn't

stupid enough to tell him that. Every night I would leave on my own, hoping to attract the attention of the right people. If I wanted to be kidnapped, I had to look as helpless as possible. The fucks hadn't taken the bait, yet, so I was left floundering for what to do. None of this would work if they didn't take me.

I sat in the VIP lounge next to Damon as we had a meeting to discuss things. Dimitri had his laptop out on the coffee table where we could hear Jensen talking over the speakers. I needed as much information as possible for when I got access to the inside.

Dimitri had finally pulled his head out of his ass, though he still sported longer hair and a beard than normal. At least he was actively trying to get his girl back. He had spoken with the boss of the trade who his father had been working with. The fucker hadn't even hidden the fact that he'd taken Cherry and was housing her. He wouldn't tell us the details, but the meeting had gotten his head back in the game.

"So, we know who has her and where she is being held. That will make things much easier. I have sent over a blueprint of the estate where Lorenzo Russo does his business here in the states." Jensen spoke over the speakers and Damon pulled up the blueprints for me to go over.

"Depending on the guard situation and security, it shouldn't be too hard to get us out of there. Tell me more about this Lorenzo guy." I said, while looking through the blueprints on the screen.

More files popped up on the screen, including photos of the man. "Lorenzo, age 39, is the head of the Cosa Nostra. He took over a few years ago after the death of his father, Antonio. His primary organization takes place in Sicily, but he's been staying here in the states for a while now while he runs things remotely. He works in everything you'd expect from someone in the mafia, but drugs and human trafficking seem to be his biggest form of business. He worked with Madax to get his foot in the door here in the states which benefited him greatly. Fucking with him might not have been the best choice."

Looking over the files and photos, it was hard to miss the fact that the man was attractive. He had dark hair and deep brown eyes. He was everything you'd expect from an Italian mob boss, from the classy suits to the tattoos on his arms.

"Is Angel's tracker still working?" Damon asked from my side.

"Yes, sir. There have been no issues or delays in her tracker. We know where she's going and we can keep an eye on her. It tracks her location and vital signs. The envelope that was given to her holds a watch. Inside the face of which is a small drive she can insert into Lorenzo's personal computer. That should give me access to everything without him ever knowing. Just remember, it takes 30 seconds to connect. Make sure the time closes before removing it," Jensen said.

I forwarded all the information to my phone and sat back on the sofa with a sigh. "Thank you, Jensen. You've been a big help."

"My pleasure, Angel." He said before signing off.

"I hope you know what you're doing," Dimitri said, packing up his things to leave.

"I promise I'll get her back, Dimitri." I hoped he believed me. Even if I didn't get out, I was going to make sure Cherry was safe and back with him. The death of Madax was on me. I'd taken him out and fucked with Lorenzo's business. She had nothing to do with it.

He tilted his head in a slight nod before walking out, leaving just me and Damon in the room.

He slipped his hand into mine, pulling me closer to him, where he forced me to face him, capturing the hair at the base of my head in a tight grip.

"You better come back too or I'll burn the fucking place down." He growled

I patted his chest lightly. "Hopefully it doesn't come to that, big guy."

He didn't waste a second as he captured my lips with his in a searing, hungry kiss. Gripping his shirt in my hand, I slipped onto his lap, straddling him. I didn't know what was going to happen once I was taken and if I never saw him again; I wanted to claim him, just like he'd claimed me.

He was already hard against my aching center as I ground myself along his impressive length. The man had no business being so fucking attractive and having such a massive dick. I was suddenly very happy that I'd picked out a skater-style dress to wear as his hands slid under the skirt to grip my hips. I made quick work unbuttoning his dress pants and freeing his dick, sliding his pocketknife from his pocket. He always had some array of weapons on his person, which was honestly really fucking hot. I sat the knife next to us on the couch as I slid my hands underneath the hem of his shirt. Filling his ab muscles tense underneath my palms.

"What do you plan to do with that, Angel?" Damon groaned against my lips as I took his dick in one of my hands, pumping him slowly.

"Let me worry about that." I lifted myself, sliding my panties to the side as I moved just the tip along my wet folds.

The small amount of friction made me moan softly. He let me tease us both for a moment before his grip on my hair tightened and he yanked my head to the side, giving him access to my neck. His lips trailed along my jaw and down my neck, biting and sucking, causing gasps to fall from my lips. I didn't know why, but I craved this man more than I'd craved anything else in my life. He'd worked his way under my skin and there was no getting rid of Damon Ashford once he sank his teeth into you. Maybe I had been an idiot to think I could just run off last time.

Positioning his cock at my entrance, I slowly slid down his length until he was fully sheathed. A deep groan left him from deep in his chest as his grip on my hips tightened, his teeth sinking into the tender flesh of my neck. I slowly began to ride him, sliding my soaking pussy almost completely up his dick before sliding back down. His head fell back against the couch as I rode him and he thrust his hips up to meet me, forcing him to hit that sweet spot deep within me. I took my time lazily unbuttoning his dress shirt to reveal the beautiful art that decorated his firm chest and abs. There was a small blank area right above his heart that would work perfectly for what I was about to do. I slowed my pace even further as I gripped the knife and flipped the blade open. I trailed it down his neck and over his nipples, being careful not to actually cut, as we continued our slow, tortuous pace. The groans and moans that left his lips had me clenching my cunt around his cock. Fuck, I loved the sounds this man-made when he was inside of me. Ever so slowly, I dragged the blade along that blank spot, letting the blade dig into his skin until a small drop of blood dripped down the surface. He groaned and I could have sworn he got even harder as he thrust into me harder.

"Be careful or you'll make me fuck it up." I tried to sound annoyed. Instead, it came out more like a breathy moan.

"Don't stop, Angel." He rasped.

I smiled as I worked the blade across his skin. Marking him just like he'd done to me. It was nice to know that he enjoyed receiving the pain just as much as he liked to dole it out. As I finished with the last letter, I leaned back slightly to admire my work. It simply read "Angel" in a crude sort of line work but I loved seeing the blood trail from the wound. I closed the knife, tossing it to the side as I leaned forward to run my tongue along the trail of blood. I moaned at the metallic taste and as soon as the sound of pleasure left my lips, Damon sprung to action. He gripped my hips forcibly as he flipped me over onto the couch and pistoned his hips even faster, driving his cock deeper into my waiting cunt. I wrapped my legs around his waist, thrusting my hips to match his thrusts, and slipped my hands into his hair, where I pulled him towards me into a searing kiss.

The kiss was just as rough as his hips, including a mix of teeth and tongue. He was devouring me in the best way, and all I wanted was more. More of this agonizing torture, more of this beautifully fucked up man who turned my world upside down. He reached down between us until his fingers found my swollen clit, where he rubbed me in slow circles without breaking the pace of his hips. The sensations had me arching my back and screaming his name as my orgasm ripped through me. He wasn't done though, and yanked me up into his arms. I gripped his shoulders to steady myself as he fucked up into me. Moving one of his hands to the front of my dress, he ripped the thin fabric down the center bearing my breasts. His mouth found my peaked nipple, and he sucked it into his mouth, biting down until I was sure he broke the skin, but I was too far gone to care as another orgasm built in the core of my stomach. I was almost certain that the first never stopped as another wave of pleasure washed over me. Damon was thorough as he worked me through my release, slowing his thrusts as I came down from the high. He released my nipple with an audible pop before running his tongue over the blood that beaded to the surface.

"I love it when you bleed for me, baby girl." He growled, thrusting his hips at a slow, hard pace.

He took the opposite nipple into his mouth, sucking gently and giving it the same attention as he had the other. His hands gripped my waist hard enough to leave bruises as he moved my hips to ride him as he thrust into me. It created the perfect amount of friction, and another orgasm built. His pure strength and drive had me aching all over again.

"Come for me again, Angel. I want every drop of your pleasure soaking my cock." He groaned deep in his throat, thrusting his hips faster. His body was tense, as if he was trying to hold himself back.

I used my hold on his shoulders to lift myself up and down his length to match his hard thrusts as my body trembled. A whimper escaped my lips as a third orgasm shot through me and he soon followed after, filling me with his come.

We were a mess as he leaned back onto the sofa, never slipping out of me. I rested my head on his shoulder as we both tried to catch our breath and admired the new mark I'd given him. The blood had begun to dry by this point, so I lightly traced my finger along the outline of the lettering. Damon's arm snaked around me, holding me close to him, and his chin rested on the top of my head.

We stayed like this for some time. Just wrapped in the other's arms and a comforting silence. I was spent, and I felt safe in his arms. I wasn't sure if I would ever be able to feel like this again, so I savored every moment. A deep-seated pity filled me the longer we stayed like this. The calm before the storm.

CHAPTER FIVE

Damon

Sitting here with Angel wrapped in my arms was like my own personal heaven. Her soft curves fit perfectly against mine and I didn't want the moment to end. I knew Angel wasn't the lovey-dovey type, and I highly doubted I'd ever get her to admit she cared about me, but she'd just marked me. She'd carved her name above my heart and staked her claim on me. Just thinking about the way she had cut into me had me growing hard inside of her again. A man could die happily buried balls deep in her warm, wet cunt.

I rested my chin on the top of her head as she curled into me. Her sweet lavender and lilac scent surrounded me. I'd fucking missed her, and I was pissed that I could lose her again. She was putting herself in danger, trying to get Cherry back. It was a good plan, but I still didn't like it. I meant what I had said. If she didn't come back, I'd go in there, guns blazing and burn the fucking place to the ground.

We stayed like this, enjoying our time together. It was nice to hold her like this. It was almost like back at the beginning, when we would spend the entire night fucking only to fall asleep in each other's arms. I wasn't sure how I was such a lucky bastard that she'd picked me to spend her time with. While she was gone, I didn't know what to do with myself. I had just spent the time stalking her every move until she had settled down.

It was almost closing time, so we got ourselves situated back into our clothes. I smiled to myself as Angel groaned when she noticed there was no fixing her dress. I hadn't meant to rip it, but her frustration afterward was well worth it.

"You owe me a new damn dress." She seethed, tying the loose sides into a knot.

It wasn't perfect, but it would be good enough for getting her home tonight without everyone on staff seeing her tits. I walked over to her, grabbed her hips to pull her flush against me, and placed light kisses along her jaw.

"You can have whatever you want, Angel. All you have to do is ask."

She huffed, rolling her eyes, and headed towards the door. Before she could make it out, I gave her plump little ass a good slap. I couldn't get enough of her.

Walking into work, I was surprised to see Dimitri sitting at the bar with a drink so early in the day. Worry ate at my gut as I made my way over and Zack just slid a tumbler of scotch in front of me. Yep, not good.

"Just spit it out," I growled, glaring at them both.

"They grabbed Angel last night," Zack said, looking over at me with worry. He pushed his phone towards me on the bar top. The video of a white van pulling up and snatching my girl was on full display.

My vision tunneled as I threw back the shot that had been offered and stormed out of the bar. I knew this had been Angel's plan, but that didn't mean I had to be happy about it. Fuck this bullshit.

CHAPTER SIX

Angel

Fuck, my head was pounding. I didn't want to open my eyes, and I felt like I'd been run over by a fucking mack truck. Groaning, I rolled over and realized I was lying on a hard mattress that reeked of human filth and mold. Or maybe that was just wherever I was.

Toto, we weren't in Kansas anymore. I opened my eyes to a dark room where it was impossible to make much out. All I could tell was that the space was dark and moldy. Wiping my hands down my face, I noticed my hands were in chains, like you'd see in those pirate movies where they wrapped around your wrists and ankles. Great. Chained up in a dark hole. I fucking hated being chained up, but that could only mean that those bastards had finally taken the bait and snatched me up.

My brain was foggy, and I couldn't remember anything after leaving the club last night. With the way my head felt and the nausea, I was sure they'd used some sort of drug to knock me out. All I could do now was wait and see how things played out.

I plopped back onto the mattress that was laid on the floor and made myself as comfortable as possible while I waited for my captors to show themselves.

I awoke with a start to the sound of a door being swung open and hitting the wall. Jumping up, I stood to face who had barged into the room. I might be chained to the wall, but like hell, if I wouldn't put up a fight. All I could see was the silhouette of a man as he entered the room. He was big and in casual clothes, from the looks of it.

"Boss wants to see you." He said in a gravelly, heavily accented voice.

Seeing the boss was probably the best way to find my way to Cherry and get us both out of here. I allowed the man to unlock my chain from the wall and followed him out of the room. It was fucking bright outside of that room. The fluorescent lights lead up a flight of stairs. Glancing around, I noticed a handful of other doors like the one I'd just walked out off. Did they really leave people in those dark holes?

Getting a good look at the man escorting me, I took in his appearance as we made our way up the stairs to a main floor that was decorated in white and grey finery. He was most likely in his late forties, with wrinkles beginning to appear on his face. He was obviously Sicilian, with tattoos on his arms, salt, and pepper hair slicked back, and a matching short beard. His brown eyes scanned the area as we walked, and he carried himself with an air of caution and confidence. Dressed in a black button-up shirt with the sleeve rolled up and a brown vest overtop. He kept the rest of his outfit casual, with a pair of tailored blue jeans and dress casual shoes. He didn't speak much, and I took the time as we walked to take in my surroundings.

The floors were made of pale grey hardwood. From the looks and feel of it, it was real hardwood as my bare feet padded quietly over the smooth surface. All the walls were a pale cream color and were decorated with beautiful monochromatic artwork. The pieces were mostly abstract, but upon closer inspection, they depicted nude men and women in erotic scenes. The place screamed money and elegance without being over the top. There were a few windows, but it appeared as if they were all sealed shut. I guess you couldn't be too careful when you kidnapped people. That took slipping through an open window out of the escape plan. I'd have to find a way for us to get out.

The man stopped at a set of grey double doors and pushed one open, letting me go in first. Walking into the room, I found an office with wall-to-wall bookshelves up the high ceiling. A modern desk sat in the middle. The top was stained dark grey and was held up by golden legs in the shape of rectangles on each side. Behind the desk, I could see a set of floor-to-ceiling curtains that were pulled closed. The chair that went with it was a dark grey wingback office chair, and my eyes snagged on the man sitting there.

He was typing away on his laptop with the screen illuminating his black-framed glasses. He was nicely tanned, showing off that he spent his time in the sun. His beard was well-groomed, fading into his dark hair. Said hair was short on the sides and long at the top, which was slicked back, and meticulously styled. His face was angular, with a straight nose that complimented the rest of his face. He was dressed in a black three-piece suit, and black leather oxford shoes, and his black and silver striped tie was loose around his neck. This man was the one and only Lorenzo Russo. The pictures that Jensen had sent didn't do this man justice. If he'd been anyone else, I'd call him attractive, but his line of work lessened the effect.

As I stopped in front of his desk with my escort behind me, I jiggled the chains on my wrists to get his attention. Have I mentioned how much I hate being chained up?

"Are these really necessary?" I asked, hoping one of these idiots would get the hint and take them off.

Lorenzo looked up from his computer screen, eyeing me from my bare feet up to my face. "I've heard that I should not underestimate you, Angel."

His Italian accent was thick, and the deep tenor was absolutely yummy. It flowed over my skin, breaking me out in goosebumps. Why were the most attractive men always the most disgusting? It would make things easier if they were fat and ugly.

"So, you know who I am?" I said, letting my arms fall in front of me. Maybe if I didn't seem like a threat, they wouldn't keep me chained up.

"I know everything about you." He stood from his chair, took his glasses off, placed them on the desk, and walked around the desk to stand in front of me. He was fucking tall, taller than Damon, and if I had to guess, he was 6'4". "Angel Hart, 28. You had a younger sister who was murdered 8 years ago. Then you took your time killing the men responsible, including my late partner Madax Ashford. You're intimate with Damon Ashford and you just got back after you had settled into a small town in North Carolina. If I were a betting man, I would assume that is due to my men taking Ms. Vahn. Am I correct?"

I glared up at him. I wouldn't give him the satisfaction of any other response. With him standing this close, I could smell his sandalwood and patchouli scent. It was a warm, comforting scent that only made me dislike him more. I wasn't sure what the best way to play this was. He obviously knew me and the things I'd done. I was a threat and a wild card. He wouldn't just let me roam and find a way out. His chocolate eyes studied me, watching my every move. He was smart, and he wouldn't be easy to fool like I'd been hoping. Fuck, what had I gotten myself into?

"So, where is Cherry?" I said, keeping my voice as calm as possible.

"She is up in a room." He sounded so matter-of-fact about that statement as he leaned against the desk, putting himself closer to my eye level. "Don't worry. She's safe and remains untouched. I only took her to prove a point to those boys that took over my late partner's affairs."

I felt my shoulders relax, knowing that nothing bad had happened to her, but I was still cautious. They obviously took us for a reason. I needed to know what he was planning. "Then what the hell do you want with us?"

"Like I said, to prove a point."

"Which would be?" He smiled at my question.

That smile was dangerous and wicked. The man was fucking charming. I'd give him that. I really didn't expect him to grab my chains and pull me flush against him. Holding me between his legs as he got in my face.

"I'm sure you'd love to know, *principessa*." He gripped my chin, using his thumb to pull down on my bottom lip. "*Hai una bocca così bella, Angel.*"

I snapped my teeth at his finger, just missing, and he pulled his hand away from my face. This fucker was going to piss me off. It made me even madder that I didn't know what the fuck he was saying. Based on the look on his face and body language, I was sure it had been suggestive in some way.

Despite my inappropriate behavior, he simply smiled at me before speaking to the other guy. "Dante…" He spoke followed by a string of Italian I had no chance in hell understanding. At least now I knew the guy's name was Dante. That much I could understand. Lorenzo pushed me back lightly so that he was standing in front of me and handed my chains to Dante. He took the chains and led me out of the room. We went up 2 flights of stairs and to the door of what I assumed was a bedroom. The grey door locked from the outside with a pin pad and I watched as Dante typed in the numbers to unlock the door.

1-3-6-8-4-2. He pushed me into the room and I staggered in. Those numbers probably wouldn't help me much, but I'd much rather be safe than sorry later on.

"Angel!"

Glancing up at my name being called, I found Cherry rushing towards me, but she stopped short as Dante stepped into the room. He made quick work of undoing my restraints before stepping back towards the door.

He glared at me, throwing the chains over his shoulder. "Don't try anything stupid. Bathroom and closet are through those doors."

I looked to where he'd pointed to see the two grey doors as he shut and locked the door. Cherry threw her arms around me, and on instinct, I hugged her back.

"Why are you here, Angel?" She asked as she roamed her eyes over me as if searching for injury while I did the same to her.

"I came to get you out. Are you okay? Have they touched you? I'm going to strangle those assholes with their intestines." She took my hand and led me over to the far side of the room where two twin-sized beds with a nightstand between them sat. She sat me on the unmade bed and took my hands in hers as she told me all that had happened.

"So they snatched me at the club a few weeks ago while I was leaving work. I woke up in a dark room in the basement before they brought me up here. I'm fine, and no one has done anything. Lorenzo is the guy that worked with Madax, but I don't think he plans on selling us. He's just trying to get back at Dimitri for ending their business agreements. I don't know much, other than Lorenzo is the guy in charge of the girls that go missing from the club. He's bad news though, and I get a really bad feeling from him."

"So, have they just been leaving you locked in here?" I asked, while looking around the room. The place was bare besides the beds with white linens, the grey nightstand with a lamp on top, and the doors that led to the closet and bathroom on the opposite wall.

"Pretty much. They bring me books and puzzles to keep me busy and food throughout the day." She glanced out of the window. "It's getting late, so they should bring dinner soon."

I got up and walked over to the window. Of course, it was sealed shut like the others. If I stayed locked up in this room, how was I going to get us out of here?

CHAPTER SEVEN

Damon

"Do you fucking know where she is?" I growled into the phone.

"Yes, she's at the estate and from the looks of it, she's been in the same room of the estate for the past week." Jensen's voice said over the speaker. It had been a week since they'd taken Angel and I wasn't handling things well.

What if she couldn't find her way out? Who knew what that fucker was doing to her? Since the news broke, I'd been dragging people into my basement. I was on edge and was ready to storm that damn building to get my girl back. This had been Angel's plan, but I didn't give a shit. I couldn't handle not knowing if she was okay.

"You have to trust she knows what she's doing," Dimitri said from his seat in front of my desk. He'd been oddly calm about all of this.

I shot a glare at him before looking back at the screen to see the blinking red dot. That was Angel. She was alive and being kept in that room. What the fuck was taking her so long to get them out of there?

"I received an invitation for us. Lorenzo is having an *event* at the estate this weekend. Maybe we will see the girls then." Dimitri said, taking a drink from his tumbler. His drinking was the only sign that something was wrong with him. He was just as stressed about the situation as I was, but he was the only person I could be mad at right now.

"I'll keep an eye on her tracker, sir. I will let you know if anything changes." Jensen said, the sound of keys typing away in the background heard over the speaker on my phone.

I didn't say anything as I hung up the phone. I was over this bullshit.

"Stop screaming like a little bitch." I growled at the man dangling from the ceiling of my basement.

He was just some low-life druggy who hadn't paid us a debt he owed. He probably didn't deserve all this, but I was in a mood. I couldn't hurt Angel. Damon had kicked me out of his office during my last meeting with him, and so fucking up this low life was the only thing I could do to keep myself calm.

He screamed as I sliced through his skin, peeling the flesh from the muscle. It was fun watching how much a human body could handle while you slowly skinned them alive. I tossed the flesh into a nearby bucket and poured a handful of salt into my palm.

"You owe us an enormous debt, Johnny. Got anything you can give to make us even?" I asked, watching the snot and tears run down the fuck's face.

Not such a big man when you were about to be food for the worms. He sniffled, screamed, and begged. There was nothing he could offer us. He was a waste of oxygen. Why Madax had kept him around and funded his addictions, I'd never understand.

The list of idiots I needed to dispose of was extensive, but they at least kept me busy. I rubbed the salt into his fresh wound and thrived on the screams of agony. Inflicting pain always made my dick hard, and I was to the point of bursting from the adrenaline pumping through my veins.

I took my time skinning the fucker until he passed out from the blood loss and pain. He'd bleed out within about five minutes. I'd been skinning him for hours. Never letting his body heal or be able to stop the blood from flowing. So I left him hanging there while I made my way to the basement shower. Before the water would warm up, I stripped out of my jeans and climbed into the shower. I let the cold water wash over me, plastering my hair to my face, neck, and back. I just stood there watching the red-stained water run down the drain.

I felt lost without her. Like a rabid beast was clawing under my skin to get out. I'd just gotten her back. She'd made progress and claimed me. How could she just be taken right after that? The thought of her in that place with my enemies was leaving me strung tight, about to break.

I'd get my girl back if it was the last thing I ever did.

CHAPTER EIGHT

Angel

Things went by slowly. Cherry and I stayed locked in this room together. We talked and caught up about life since I'd left, played board games, put together puzzles, and did anything to keep ourselves busy. I was fucking bored and found myself agitated as the week went on.

A week. I'd been locked in this fucking room for a week. The only people I saw were Cherry and Dante when he brought us our meals. I was so over this bullshit. I didn't get how she'd been able to stand it and stay her usual bubbly self. Granted, she wasn't happy, but she was handling things so well. I knew things could be much worse for us, but I still couldn't stand being a prisoner. We had a closet full of clothes and shoes with a fully stocked bathroom. Overall, we were fed and taken care of.

As of now, Cherry was sitting on her bed putting together a 500-piece puzzle and I was lying on mine reading some sort of rom-com, contemporary romance that she'd recommended. It was the story of some literary agent who goes off to a small town and falls in love with an editor she's had a grudge against. It's a good read and I find myself lost in the story. I wouldn't have picked it for myself.

Romance isn't my thing, if my *relationship* with Damon is any indication. When did I even start referring to it as a relationship? There must be something in the fucking water here because I'm not into all that romance shit. I guess I miss the brute, though. We'd had a good thing last time I was in town and things had picked up again fairly quickly as soon as I walked back through the doors of Hellfire. I really needed to get out of here if that was the way my brain was working.

A knock came at the door before Dante walked in. He was dressed in his usual style of blue jeans, a pair of loafers, and had on a white button-up dress shirt. I'd come to learn that while he dressed nicely, he also liked a bit of casual comfort. He didn't speak to us much outside of making sure we didn't need anything. He walked over to my side of the bed and that's when I noticed the handcuffs in his hand. I guess the plus side was that it was just a standard pair of cuffs.

"*Il Capo*, would like to speak with you, Ms. Hart." He said, holding his hand out for me to take. They switched between Italian and English, so it didn't take me long to pick up that il capo meant *the boss*. I still couldn't understand the shit Dante said sometimes, but I at least got it.

I eyed the cuffs in his hand while placing my book face down on the bed. "Are those really necessary?"

"*Sí.*"

A man of few words. I rolled my eyes before throwing my legs over the side of the bed and standing in front of him. I held my wrists out as he secured the cuffs before walking out the door. Cherry was quiet as he escorted me out of the room and locked the door behind us.

He led me back downstairs to the same office as before. I took note of every turn and even noticed the front entryway was unguarded. Maybe that could be our way out. Yeah, going out the front door probably wasn't the best choice, but it was the only option I'd seen since we'd been here. I'd need to see more of the place if I was going to figure out a way to get Cherry out of here, hopefully getting myself out too.

Like before, he opened the door to the office and motioned for me to go in first. The only difference this time was that the large window behind the desk had the curtains drawn, allowing the bright sunshine to fill the space. I walked directly up to the desk, my hands bound in front of me, and glared at the man sitting there on his computer. Lorenzo glanced up at me and smiled that charming smile of his.

"Angel, I'm glad you could come to speak with me." He trailed his eyes over my body. I'd been in a pair of black Soffe shorts and a white tank top and I hadn't bothered to change for this.

"I didn't realize I had a choice." I presented my bound hands with a classic eye roll. This dude really got on my nerves.

Lorenzo stood and walked around the desk to stand in front of me again. He grabbed hold of my chin, forcing me to look up into his warm, chocolate eyes, "*Dante, dacci un po' di privacy.*"

Maybe figuring out some of what they said wouldn't be too hard. All I understood the words were meant for Dante and based on privacy; he was telling him to leave just us in this room. While Dante slipped out of the office, I didn't take my eyes off Lorenzo as I glared up at him. What the hell did this fucker want?

"You are absolutely stunning, *principessa.*" He said, trailing that thumb over my bottom lip again.

His free hand gripped my bound wrists, and the hand slid from my face as he reached into his pocket, extracting a key. He didn't waste a second as he unlocked my cuffs and dropped them and the key on the desk.

"I am trusting you not to do anything rash, *principessa.*" He said, walking back to sit in his chair.

I stood there and rubbed my wrists while watching his every move. I didn't understand the point of all this. Was he trying to gain my trust or play some sort of fucked up game?

"What do you want, Lorenzo?" I asked.

He simply smiled, folding his hands under his chin as he leaned forward on the desk. "Please call me Enzo."

"Whatever. What do you want, *Enzo*?" I growled out between clenched teeth.

His eyes seemed to shine as he looked me over, his gaze lingering on my lips. "There are a few things I want."

"Care to elaborate? Or is this going to be a pointless conversation?"

"I would like to have my old partnership back with Ashford Enterprise. I would also like to have you." He said all of this matter of factually while I just stood there contemplating his words. There was no way Dimitri would start up a partnership with him. He hated the skin trade and made it his mission to get rid of that part of the business when Madax was out of the picture. He would do anything to get Cherry back, though, even cutting a deal with Lorenzo if he needed. I was sure I could play this in my favor and find some way to screw over this asshole standing in front of me.

"The only way you're getting that deal back is if you give Cherry back to Dimitri. Until then, he won't be interested in striking any sort of deal with you." I purposely didn't mention the fact that he'd just admitted that he wanted me, as if I were some piece of property meant to be bought and sold. The thought had my blood boiling. This guy was a fucking monster.

"Fair point. This weekend, I am hosting an event here at my home. I have taken the liberty of inviting Mr. Ashford and his brother. Ms. Vahn is free to leave with them that evening on one condition." His smile turned almost mocking.

"What condition?" I already knew what he would say.

"He will sign a legal contract with me that night and you stay here with me, under full watch, of course. You will be free to do as you please, so long as you remain here on the grounds, *principessa*." His expression was smug now as he watched me shift my weight uncomfortably.

"Deal, but I'm sure you'll be disappointed." I crossed my arms over my chest, glancing over at the books that lined the walls.

"We shall see."

CHAPTER NINE

Angel

The weekend came quickly and in the late afternoon, a parade of people came into the room to get us ready for whatever event they were having. They got to work on Cherry first. They left her short blonde hair down in elegant waves and applied a light layer of makeup that didn't cover up her natural, innocent beauty. She looked stunning as they led her into our walk-in closet to find the perfect dress and shoes for the evening.

I hadn't told her yet that she'd be going home tonight while I stayed behind. I'd thought out a plan that could work in everyone's favor. For now, though, I needed to focus on my end of the bargain I had struck with Lorenzo. Things could get messy if everything didn't go exactly right.

asking for my opinion on looks. I obviously only had one request, a bold red lipstick. I needed the confidence boost if I was going to play my part tonight.

Lorenzo hadn't given me details of what the event actually was, but I was unaware I'd be showing up on his arm. I had been instructed to do everything he asked without question and to enjoy myself. Most of all, I couldn't make a scene or he wouldn't let Cherry leave. Every instinct was telling me to stab him in the gut, but I couldn't force a slave life on the closest person I'd had to being an actual friend. She needed to get back to Dimitri and Zack. I'd figure out how to get myself out of this situation.

Hopefully.

When the woman was finished with my hair and makeup, I looked into the mirror to see a silver smokey eye that made my blue eyes appear even bluer. She'd used black eyeliner to create a winged cat eye effect, giving the perfect siren eye look. The face makeup was light to appear natural and the red lipstick was fairly close to my go-to shade. I could already tell it was just regular lipstick and not a stain like I was used to. I'd have to be careful not to have this one streaked across my face. The older lady had even left the lipstick for me on the nightstand in case I'd need to reapply it. My hair was placed up into a low, elegant bun at the base of my neck, with curled pieces of midnight hair framing my face.

By the time the woman was satisfied with how I looked, Cherry was walking out of the closet in a mid-calf length dress. It was pale blue, and the fabric held a light shimmer to it. It fitted to her frame with a slight flare at the hips, with a cottage core short sleeve neckline. She'd paired it with a pair of silver strappy heels. With her, they were definitely going for a light, innocent look. It suited her and her personality, and I was glad she was going to get out of this situation. If she didn't get out now, Lorenzo wouldn't keep treating us so well. I didn't want her to face the dark side of what Lorenzo was a part of. It would break her. I could handle it all on my own if it meant she got out tonight.

I assured the women fussing over us I could pick my dress as I made my way into the closet. I lightly ran my hand over the array of colorful dresses. Like hell, if I was going to be wearing something so colorful tonight. No, bright wasn't my style. I went to the drawers that housed underwear and picked out a black lace bra and thong set, slipping them on. The lace bra held my breasts up, giving me a fuller look than I actually had.

I took my time going through the dresses until I found the perfect one in black. It was floor length with a flared shirt and a slit up to the mid-thigh. The bodice was draped in lace and the v-neck dipped down between my breasts to show off a good amount of cleavage, showcasing the floral and moon sternum tattoo I'd gotten as soon as I ended up in my new life. Its long, lace sleeves fell to the back of my hands in the shape of a V and the see-through material showed off the ink on my arms. To finish the look, I added a pair of black strappy heels.

When the woman finally left the room, I sat down on the bed next to Cherry, taking her hand in mine as I slipped her a piece of paper. "Cherry, you're getting out of here tonight and leaving with Dimitri. I need you to give this note to him and Damon."

"What about you?" She nearly screeched at me. I fought the urge to cover her mouth, afraid someone could be listening.

"I'll find another way out. Tonight, when you see Dimitri, I need you to give him this note immediately. You're getting out of here depends on it.

He has to do things exactly what this note says or we are all fucked." I gripped her hands tightly, hoping that she'd do as I asked without complaint, "No matter what, make sure Dimitri and Damon do as the note says. I'm not sure what will happen if they don't."

I didn't like keeping things from her. I knew exactly what would happen to us both if the boys didn't do what needed to be done. We'd be just another set of girls who went missing and are then sold off to some sick old fuck, or worse. She nodded, tears filling her eyes as she took the note and slipped it into the top of her dress. Tonight was going to be a long night.

CHAPTER TEN

Angel

I was feeling anxious as Dante escorted us down to the event. From the sound of things, there was already a large crowd behind the double doors. This was a new area of the house, so I kept an eye out for where the guards were and any exits. I couldn't be too careful. Regardless of what transpired here tonight, Cherry was going home. I'd kill whoever I had to in order to make that happen.

Lorenzo was standing at the double doors, speaking to the guards off to the side, when he noticed us approaching. He greeted Dante with a slight nod before turning to Cherry.

"You look absolutely radiant, Ms. Vahn." He said, kissing the back of her hand. She was quick to pull her hand free and take a step back from him.

Dante presented her with his arm as he led her through the doors as Lorenzo made his way to me. Even in these tall ass heels, I had to look up at him as he stood in front of me. He gripped my waist, pulling me flush against him. His sandalwood and patchouli scent surrounded me as he placed a light kiss on my cheek.

He whispered against my skin in Italian, trailing his free hand up my throat to my chin.

"You realize I have no clue what the fuck you're saying." Even I sounded snarky to my own ears, but it only seemed to delight him as he flashed that charming smile.

"You will learn, *principessa*. Now watch your tone and behave this evening." He offered me his arm. I slipped my hand onto his arm as he escorted me inside. Even though all I wanted to do was slam the heel of these stupid shoes into his eye socket.

The place was packed, and I was shocked at what was before me. I had been expecting something similar to what Madax had taken me to the last time I was at an *event*, but this was something completely different. The area was covered in plush couches and there was sex equipment spread out around the room. There was a mix of nude bodies, men in suits, and women in fabulous gowns, watching others in an array of positions. It was an orgy, a sex dungeon placed into the middle of an extravagant ballroom.

I was sure my jaw would have ended up on the floor if I hadn't been so tense. Scanning the room, my eyes caught on Cherry standing next to Dimitri in a corner, but my eyes immediately zeroed in on the brute of a man standing next to them. Damon. His long hair was tied up in a sleek bun at the base of his neck, his beard looking a bit more grown out than the last time I'd seen him. He was dressed in an all-black suit with a deep red tie. His eyes were already on me as Lorenzo led me through the crowd. Even from this distance, I could tell he hadn't been sleeping well with the dark circles under his eyes. Every bone in my body was screaming at me to run to him. To the safety and comfort, he provided me. My heart felt like it was in a vise.

"Don't worry, *principessa*. You'll get to speak with him soon enough." Lorenzo whispered in my ear.

I tore my eyes away from Damon to look at Lorenzo. I didn't like the way he said that. It was as if there was a hidden meaning behind it. With him, it wouldn't surprise me. I glanced back at Damon as Lorenzo led me to one scene at the far end of the room.

On a platform there was a woman tied to a St. Andrew's Cross and a man in tight leather pants and a mask was whipping her with a cat-o'-nine-tails. Looking closely, I noticed a glazed look over the girl's eyes. She was drugged. Her moans filled the air every time she was struck. I didn't know if it was self-inflicted or if she'd just been given the drugs to be easier to control, but considering the shit, I knew Lorenzo was a part of I'd have to go with the latter.

We made our way around the room, Lorenzo speaking to people here and there as he showed me all the different scenes going on. It would have been hot if the people weren't being forced into their performances. The last scene we came across was of a woman being railed by two men. It appeared as if they were all into it, even though each participant shared that glazed look as they fucked each other.

"Do you like what you see, *principessa*?" Lorenzo asked as he stood behind me, rubbing my arms lightly.

"What I see are a bunch of drugged sex slaves who are being forced into a shitty lifestyle." I didn't care if it pissed him off. Honestly, I wanted to make him regret wanting to keep me.

My sass didn't seem to faze him as he chuckled, grabbed my hand, and led me out of the room. It was so quiet out in the hall in comparison. "Where are you taking me?"

He didn't answer me until he led me into a separate room. The walls were painted a deep red and the four-poster bed was covered in black silk with tulle drapery. Along the walls were drawers and everything you'd expect to be in a sex room hung along the walls. Walking around, I ran my hand lightly over floggers, whips, and many other things. I had no clue what they were used for. I heard the door clicking shut before Lorenzo made his way over to me.

"Why bring me here? You've made it clear that if I *misbehave,* you won't let Cherry leave." I looked everywhere but at him as I made my way around the room.

"Because I have a surprise for you, *principessa*." A knock sounded at the door. "Ah, and there it is. Come in."

For the millionth time, it felt like tonight I was shocked to see Damon enter the room. What the fuck was he doing here? I glanced over at Lorenzo, who simply smiled as he took off his suit jacket and loosened his tie.

He took a seat on one of the chairs facing the bed before he elaborated, "You're mine now, *principessa*. I thought it would be nice for you to have one last parting moment with your lover."

Looking at Damon, he seemed just as surprised as I was. He didn't take his eyes off me, though. It was as if he were trying to memorize every single feature of me. The way his gaze heated as he looked over my body. That warm feeling I always got from his stares washed over me. God, I had missed him this past week. I looked back at Lorenzo with a glare.

"What's the fucking catch, *Enzo*?" I was pissed off and seething.

He ignored me as he focused on Damon. "Has your brother agreed to the deal?"

"Yes," was Damon's gruff reply. His deep voice sent goosebumps over my skin. I was cold and heated all at the same time.

Lorenzo smiled and motioned towards the bed. Damon looked between me and it. He was just as unsure about all of this as I was, apparently. I kept my glare trained on Lorenzo. The charming smile hadn't left his face. I'd never wanted to hurt someone simply to cause them pain as I did that man.

He finally decided to answer me, "I'd like to watch, *principessa*, maybe join if I am so inclined. Pretend like I'm not even here."

Damon shut the door and finally walked over to me, his hand slipping around the back of my neck to pull me close to him. I sighed as his sweet mahogany scent enveloped me and I melted into his touch. I wasn't sure about all this, but damn if I was going to give up my possible last chance of being with him. His other hand gripped my waist as our bodies molded together. His thumb worked for slow, soothing circles on my hip.

"Hello, Angel." He growled through his teeth so that only I could hear. I couldn't get a read on him, which bothered me. Usually, I could read him so easily, and use his mood to my advantage, but it was as if I were seeing him now for the first and final time.

"Damon," I meant to sound more confident, but his name tumbled from my lips like a prayer. I hoped that Cherry had given them my note. That Damon had read the part specifically for him. It would have explained everything. I didn't want

Damon to think I was doing this to get away from him again. The short distance had made me realize just how wrong I'd been to leave him behind.

CHAPTER ELEVEN

Damon

Dimitri, Zack, and I had just arrived at the *party* Lorenzo was throwing. It wasn't our first time at one of his events, so we knew we'd be walking into a sexcapade. The place was full and there were different scenes going on around the room. People were placing bids on those participating in scenes. Where the old fuck had done auctions, Lorenzo did things a bit differently. He wanted to show off the skills of the people he was selling.

Dimitri was tense next to me as he scanned the area. He was sure we'd walk in to find Cherry forced into one of the scenes and drugged like the others. He gave an audible sigh of relief when it was clear she wasn't being sold or on one of the stages around the room.

"Thank goodness she isn't being forced into this mess." Zack said from next to me.

Looking at him, his eyes had snagged on a little redhead who was strapped to a cross being whipped. From the look of pity on his face, I knew the kid was about to do something stupid. But I had more to worry about than what he was thinking. We stood off to the side, watching as the night began. My eyes swept the floor for any sign of my girl. Still nothing. Lorenzo wasn't even in attendance, so things hadn't really gotten started.

"Fuck," I glanced at Dimitri to see his eyes wide, staring off to the far side of the room.

Following his gaze, I understood what had caught his attention. Cherry was being escorted in on the arm of Lorenzo's men. They were heading straight for us. Cherry's face lit up as they approached and once she was close enough, she leaped into my brother's arms. He looked her over frantically, asking if she was okay, which she reassured him she was. The guy, Dante, I believe his name was, just walked off. That was either a very good or very bad sign. Once hellos had been exchanged between everyone, Cherry handed a note to Dimitri.

"Angel said that you two needed to read it. She said it was important and couldn't wait."

Dimitri opened the note, but I couldn't pay any mind as Angel walked into the room on Lorenzo's arm. Yeah, that note was definitely bad fucking news. At least for me, anyway. My gut was rarely wrong. As soon as my girl was in the room, her eyes took in everything. She'd always been the type to scope out a situation, and she knew where everything was in a room. Her eyes stopped roaming as she looked directly at me. The fire that always consumed me when she was around fired up again. For the first time since she'd been taken, I felt fucking alive.

She was dressed in a sexy as hell black gown, and I couldn't help but want to tear it off of her delicate skin. I watched as she stayed on Lorenzo's arm and he escorted her around the room. Every now and then, he would whisper something to her to grab her attention. Her gaze always found its way back to me.

"Damon, this isn't good." Dimitri said, handing me the note.

Glancing his way, I noticed that Zack wasn't with us anymore as I took the note. Reading over it, I wanted to crumple it up and kill something.

Dimitri, I cut a deal to get Cherry out. Lorenzo wants to start up a new contract with you. The same one that Madax had with him. In exchange, he's willing to let Cherry go. Don't worry, she's been safe and taken care of. I'm not sure what he'd originally planned, but things must have changed when they took me. Part of the deal was that she could go, but I had to stay.

Just do what he asks of you. It won't stick. I have

a plan. Keep in contact with Jensen. I'll send him

everything I can to take this fucker down.

Damon, remember what you said to me. Make it

a promise. I only ask that you give me some time

to get as much information as I can. A month

tops. Just in case things don't work out like I

want, make sure you take them all out.

I know this is shitty to do this way. I should have

said it sooner, but I'm yours, Damon, and always will be.

-Angel

Now I was fucking pissed. She would never

say that shit to me. I knew her. She wasn't the

romantic type and if she was saying this in a letter;

she wasn't planning on making it out of here. My

blood boiled as I crumpled up the letter and handed it

back to Dimitri.

CHAPTER TWELVE

Angel

"You're mine, Angel," Damon whispered so that only I could hear it.

I almost melted at that. He'd gotten my letter. Shit, he'd gotten my letter. I'd admitted my feelings for him in a fucking letter. What the fuck had I been thinking? I couldn't take it back now, and this was going to be my last moment with him.

"Yours," As the word left my lips, he crashed his lips to mine.

The world faded to just us as I focused on Damon. He forced his tongue into my mouth, using his hand in my hair to angle me exactly how he wanted. His hungry kiss consumed me and I slipped my fingers into his hair, pulling him closer to me as he devoured me. This kiss was hot and desperate, and

I couldn't get him close enough. My hands slipped down his shoulder to his chest, where I wasted no time at all working my way through his buttons. My hands roamed his bare chest as his lips trailed down my chin and neck, biting and sucking on my skin. I moaned his name. He knew exactly what to do with my body to make me tick.

"Damon, why don't you get undressed and lie on the bed?"

My eyes shot to Lorenzo. What the fuck happened to pretending he wasn't here? Now he was going to order us around like his little fucking playthings. I wanted to stab him in his fucking face. Damon's hands tightened on me as he straightened, glaring at Lorenzo just like I was. He wasn't the type to be bossed around, and I could see the rage shimmering in his crystal blue eyes.

Pressing my lips to his bare chest, I whispered, "Just do what he says. I'm not sure how to play all this in our favor, but until Cherry is out of

here, you have to listen to him."

I felt his body relax to my touch before he

stepped away just enough to undress. Without taking

his eyes off me, he loosened his tie enough to slip over

his head, tossing it over onto a nearby sex bench. I

really hoped the shit in here had been cleaned. Next

to go was his suit jacket and shirt. His muscles

rippled as he moved, showing off all the ink that I

loved and the healing wound where I'd carved my

name into his chest.. I couldn't keep my hands off

him as I ran my fingers along the jagged lines of my

name over his heart. It was healing nicely, considering

it had only been a week. Damon removed his belt,

sliding it through the loops of his pants, then tossing

it over with the rest of his clothes. I lightly kissed

where I'd marked him as I replaced his hands with

mine to unbutton his pants, sliding them and his

boxers down his toned ass and thighs. As I pushed

them down farther, I trailed my lips down his body. He adjusted his stance as he slipped his shoes off and then stepped out of his pants for me. The tattoos covering this man's body always had me feeling feral. I wanted to trace every single one with my tongue. To trail my lips and tongue up his thighs to his hard cock. I might be overly responsive to him, but I was sure by now that the feelings were mutual.

I slid my tongue up the underside of his length, glancing up at him through my lashes. His hands slipped into my hair, gripping tightly to the strands as I took the head of his dick into my mouth. I sucked lightly, taking my time as he thrust his hips forward. I gripped the back of his thigh with one hand and used the other to massage his balls as I took him further into my throat. He groaned, thrusting his hips harder, which forced me to take him deeper. I hollowed my cheeks, sucking him harder as he began to fuck my face. As saliva leaked down my chin and his hands held me in place, I took everything he gave me. I wanted to taste him on my tongue, but Lorenzo had other plans as he cleared his throat. Damon pulled out of my mouth with an audible pop. If looks could kill, Lorenzo would be dead by now.

I stood up from where I'd kneeled down in front of Damon and watched as he strutted to the bed. He sat on the edge and leaned back on his elbows, and kept his eyes trained on me. Lorenzo stood from his chair and walked over to me. Taking a hold of my chin, he ran his thumb over the bottom of my lips.

"I'd hoped I would have been the one to ruin this lipstick tonight, *principessa*." I'd almost forgotten that the lipstick was there.

"I'm sure you'll have plenty of other chances." If he lived long enough, anyway, I wasn't an idiot. I knew what he had planned for me after tonight.

He smiled at me before walking behind me. He turned me to face Damon as he unzipped the back of my dress, pushing it down from my shoulders as his lips trailed along my neck and shoulder. I slipped my arms from the sleeves and let the dress pool around my feet. My eyes didn't leave Damon's as Lorenzo's lips trailed across my skin. He made a noise of approval as his fingers traced the lines of my bra and panties. The look on Damon's face was a mix of hunger and blood lust. He didn't want Lorenzo touching me, but there wasn't much we could do in this situation. Lorenzo's fingers were graceful as he unhooked my bra, and the flimsy lace joined my dress on the floor. He wasted no time slipping off my panties as well, leaving me in just the heels. As he straightened behind me, pulling my back flush against his front, his hand trailed down my stomach to my core. He began slowly fingering me as Damon watched from the bed. How did we keep getting into these situations?

"*Fottere*, she gets so wet for you, Damon." He breathed into my ear as his fingers stroked my clit. I wished it didn't feel as good as it did.

I was glad when he removed his fingers from me and I let out a breath I didn't realize I'd been holding. I heard a groan from Lorenza and heard him suck on what I assumed were his fingers.

"She tastes even sweeter than she smells." He said, letting his hands slide down my arms. His breath cascaded over my neck and an unintentional shiver wracked down my spine. "He's hard for you, *principessa*. Why don't you go ride him until he comes in that sweet pussy of yours?"

I felt a mix of sadness, disgust, and desire as I walked towards Damon on the bed. He sat up straighter as I approached, slipping his hands on my hips as I straddled his lap. He was still so fucking hard, and I wished this was happening under better circumstances. I wanted him. I just didn't want Lorenzo as an audience.

My thoughts halted when Damon reached between us to cup my core, slipping his fingers into me at a leisurely pace. "Fuck me, Angel. Use me to make your pussy weep."

A moan slipped past my lips. Fuck, I loved when he said shit like that. So possessive and controlling. While with anyone else, some of the shit he said would just piss me off. Not Damon. His words and the feel of his hands set me aflame. Like all he cared about was me. I decided to try not to think about things too much. I wanted out of my head for a while, and Damon had always been the best way to quiet my mind.

I kissed him hungrily, slipping my hands into his hair and releasing it from its tie. I loved his long hair and gripped the strands in my hands. He continued his ministrations, fucking me with his skilled fingers and kissing me back just as furiously. His mouth captured my moans of pleasure as he worked me quickly to orgasm. I shattered, toppling over the edge so fast I lost my breath. No one knew my body better than Damon.

"That's my good little slut," He praised, removing his fingers from my cunt to position his cock at my entrance.

A whimper left my lips as he thrust upward, filling me up in one fluid motion. His hands found my hips, moving me on his hard erection. "Ride me, Angel. Make me feel that greedy cunt strangle my cock."

His name fell from my lips in a breathless moan as I began to ride him, lifting myself up before sliding back down his length. The feeling of him inside of me and the dirty words he whispered had me aching for him. If he kept that up, there was no way I was going to last very long.

His mouth found my breast as I rode him and he sucked the hardened peak into his mouth, biting just the way I liked. He knew just how to mix pain in with pleasure and my body sang for him. He moved one of his hands around to work my clit as I rode him, giving me the perfect amount of friction. I was so close to another release and from the sounds Damon was making; he was too.

"That's right, Angel. Just like that." He moaned against my chest, moving to the other nipple to give it the same attention he had the other.

We were so lost in each other that I almost didn't notice when Lorenzo came up behind me, slipping a slick finger over my backside, down to my ass. In my surprise, I stopped riding Damon as my body tensed, and not in a good way. Lorenzo pushed me forward into Damon as he got a better angle on my ass.

Damon leaned back, pulling me with him as he placed a light kiss on my lips. "Eyes on me, baby girl."

His whisper was so quiet I almost missed it. He crashed his lips onto mine and began to thrust up into me. His pace was slow, almost soothing as Lorenzo lubed up my ass, slipping his fingers into my back entrance at the same pace. I moaned against Damon's lips while my body remained tense. The only person who had ever had me like that was Damon. I didn't want this. Almost as quickly as it started, Lorenzo removed his hands from me, and I heard the deafening sound of his belt and pants being undone. Damon bit my lip, trying to draw my focus to him as he went back to stimulate my clit with his finger as Lorenzo's hands found my waist. I'm sure my face was a mix of disgust and anger. Damon was doing everything he could to keep my focus on him, regardless of the same anger burning in his eyes. At that moment, I knew that one of us would be putting an end to Lorenzo Russo.

Without warning, Lorenzo pushed into my ass. His thrusts were slow at first and he would thrust into me at the same time Damon was pulling out. I had never felt so full in my fucking life. A wave of pain and pleasure ripped through me as they both fucked me. Their massive cocks slid into me at a perfect rhythm, their dicks rubbing each other from inside of me. They both groaned out in pleasure as their thrusts slowly increased in pace.

All I could do was grab onto Damon's muscular shoulders and take what they were giving me. They were slamming into me in tandem. The sounds of wet flesh and our combined sounds of pleasure filled the room until I was screaming out my release. My vision tunneled as they continued to fuck me, filling me to a point of combusting. Another orgasm overtook me, one after the other, as I dug my nails into Damon's flesh. I watched with blurry vision as Damon threw his head back and roared out his release. His cock twitched inside of me as he filled me to the brim. Lorenzo soon followed, cursing in Italian as he filled my ass with his come. As soon as he stilled, he slowly pulled from my ass, walking over to one of the doors where he pulled out a cloth to clean himself up with. I was fucking spent as I collapsed onto Damon's chest. He wrapped his arms around me, holding me to him as if he thought I'd break. We were both breathless, and I didn't want to leave the safety of his arms.

This shit was a fucking nightmare.

CHAPTER THIRTEEN

Damon

This shit was fucked. I had been escorted out of the fucking place as soon as Lorenzo was done with his fucking power trip. While it had been enjoyable being with Angel, I was pissed that the fucker had been the one in control of what was going on.

Angel had just lain there afterward. A blank look washed over her features. If she'd been the crying type, I'm sure she would have been in that moment. I'd taken my time to hold her while Lorenzo had left the room to get himself cleaned up, and I took care of my girl. She hadn't said a word the entire time. She'd retreated inside of herself, so I did the only thing I could do at that moment. I held her in my arms and talked to her. Hoping that at the very least, she'd been listening.

As soon as Lorenzo came back, I was told to get dressed and a group of guards walked me out the front door. Every fiber of my being was screaming at me not to leave her there, but she'd asked for a month to get herself out. I would give her that. Not a fucking day more. A part of me hoped that I'd be the one to end that sorry son of a bitch.

Dimitri, Cherry, Zack, and that little red head were waiting out front with our car. I couldn't even care fucking less that we had some slaver bitch with us. I didn't fucking care about right now other than Angel being stuck here.. All I saw was red, and killing Lorenzo Russo was the only thing on my mind.

"Don't tell me to fucking calm down!" I roared at Zack and Cherry.

They'd been on my ass since coming back from that fucked up party. Every day, they hounded me. Asking if I was okay when they arrived at the club. Dimitri had stuck close to Cherry since getting her back, so he'd spent most evenings that she'd worked sitting at the bar. He'd done nothing to stop the insistent line of questions from the twins. I was going to end up murdering them all.

"Damon, we are going to get her back. If anyone can get out of that place, it's Angel. She's been scoping out the place since she showed up. Keeping an extensive record of everything, including when guards were patrolling outside of our window. She'd checked and all the windows were sealed shut. She'll come up with some way to get out. I'm sure of it." Cherry was always so fucking positive about everything. I just didn't want to hear any of it.

I threw the keys to Hellfire on the bar in front of Dimitri and walked out. I'd ridden my bike today, and I just needed to get out of there. I'd gotten word that there were some fights going on in the next town over and I was going to need to draw some blood if I was going to be stuck fucking waiting around for the next month.

CHAPTER FOURTEEN

Angel

I'd woken the next morning after the event in my little prison cell. Everything was sore, and I just wanted to stay buried in these blankets for the next month. Fuck this bullshit.

I didn't even remember anything after Damon had pulled me into his arms last night. I really didn't want to think about what had happened. This had been my idea. I'd taken the deal Lorenzo had offered me, so all of it was on me. Looking over at Cherry's bed, I noticed that it was empty and unused. At least she'd gotten out. That was what mattered the most. Cherry was safe and with her family again. Now I just needed to focus on surviving this hell I'd gotten myself into.

I wasn't doing shit until I could get out of my own head. I pulled the covers over my head and went back to sleep.

Three days went by where I simply stayed in bed. I didn't worry about showering and I hardly touched the food that Dante would bring me. I was thankful that I hadn't had to face Lorenzo yet. Dante had even informed me I was free to roam the house, so long as I stayed on the grounds. I was a prisoner, but one who had a leash.

I finally decided it was time to stop sulking and get a plan together. I needed to find a way to take down Lorenzo's business from the inside and get rid of him. We didn't need another him swooping in to cause problems later on down the road. It had to be clean, and we had to have someone in power that we could trust. I was sure that Jensen would know what to do once I gave him access to the information he needed, anyway.

Thanks to the notebooks they'd provided Cherry before I got here, I was able to write down everything I learned and did. I needed there to be a record in case I didn't make it out. I knew Damon would come storming this place as soon as my month was up and he'd need the information to keep things running smoothly or hand things over to Dimitri, anyway. Things could get messy fast if I wasn't careful.

I slipped out of bed and decided three days was long enough to lie around without taking care of myself. Grabbing a pair of black sweatpants and a white sports bra before heading into the shower to make myself more presentable, in case I ran into Lorenzo while I looked around. I still wanted to dress for comfort. I didn't know if I'd need to fight off some asshole in this place.

Aside from the occasional guard, the place was quiet as hell. I wasn't sure who all stayed here. I was curious if the others I'd seen at the party over the weekend were housed here or somewhere else. Brushing the thought away as I walked the halls, I took in the erotic abstract that was scattered around the place. Why did rich pricks have to flaunt their money and have these big ass houses? It seemed like a waste, considering every large house I'd ever been in was completely empty. It would have made more sense if they had a big family or some shit like that.

My search led me to find absolutely nothing of interest. Every window was sealed shut and the only exits were the front and back doors. Why couldn't shit just be easy so that I could get out quickly? I found my way back to Lorenzo's office and opened the door a crack. To my surprise, it was empty, so I slipped in, shutting the door behind me. The laptop Lorenzo always used was sitting there open on the desk, so I did the only logical thing in this situation. Once seated at the desk, I took off my watch, popped the face-off, and extracted the small flash drive. I tossed it into the slot on the computer and a countdown bar appeared, counting down from thirty seconds. While that was going, I started looking through all of Lorenzo's files. I wasn't the most tech savvy, but I'd learned a couple of handy things over the years to cover my tracks. When you spent eight years stalking and killing people, you had to learn to do certain things.

The files were all about his business. It took me a bit, but I was finally able to find something of use. I quickly opened up a secure email and proceeded to attach the files to the message just in case this drive or whatever didn't work like it was supposed to. Jensen had made sure I knew how to contact him if I was ever able to do so. There were files of all Lorenzo's contacts, offshore account information, where he held his "stock" prior to their sale, and a couple of files containing sensitive information about many of those involved in Lorenzo's unsavory adventures. After sending the email, I quickly wiped any trace that I'd been there and made sure everything was exactly how Lorenzo left it. The driver had finished doing its thing by the time I was done snooping. I took it from the computer, slipping it back into the hidden compartment of my watch. I wasn't sure if what I'd sent would be helpful for the guys, but I was confident they could figure shit out for themselves. They'd been in this business a lot longer than me and had smart people at their disposal.

Standing from the desk, I decided to see what books I could find in Lorenzo's personal collection. If I was stuck here, I might as well find something to do with my time. I'd just found a fairly interesting collection of poetry when the door clicked open. I didn't bother to look back as I scanned through the book in my hands.

Soft footsteps echoed across the floor and stopped behind me. I had to remind myself not to act out of character as I flipped to the next page. The worst thing I could do would be to act like I'd been snooping and sticking my nose where it didn't belong. Soft fingertips brushed along my arm as the other snaked around my waist, pulling me back into a muscular body. Where Damon was rough and calloused, Lorenzo was hard muscle and soft skin. He reminded me of Dimitri in that aspect. He was clean cut and rarely got his hands dirty. Definitely not my type.

"What are you doing, *principessa?*" His soft Italian accent brushed along my shoulder.

"Looking for something to do. I'm bored and I'm tired of reading romance." I placed the book back in its spot, picking up another to flip through.

His lips brushed over where my neck met my shoulder. "Ah, so you aren't the romantic type?"

I chuckled darkly, pulling out of his arms to put the book back and face him. He was dressed in a pair of heather grey slacks, a black button-up shirt, and black leather shoes. His shirt was undone at the top to show his chest and sleeves rolled up to show off a scattering of tattoos on his forearms.

"Romance and love aren't my thing," I said, studying him to get his reaction.

He simply smiled at me, taking my chin between his fingers as he closed the distance between us. "What can I do to change your mind? I don't believe wooing you is the right way to earn your affections."

"I didn't realize earning my affection was part of your game. I'm simply a prisoner in a pretty cage."

I really needed to learn how to keep my snark to myself. His eyes hardened on me and the smile dropped from his face. Yep. He didn't like to be sassed. He slipped his hand from my chin into the hair at the nape of my neck, jerking my head back.

"I do not appreciate your tone."

He twirled me around to face the desk, pushing me over the top by my hair as he used his other hand to lower my panties and sweatpants. Lorenzo didn't waste any time pushing them down farther than he needed and a zipper being undone filled my ears. Fuck if he was going to have me without a fight.

Using my hands, I pushed off the desk and kicked my foot back, making contact with his leg. He grunted as I scurried away from him. Pulling my pants up as I went. I didn't get far. I hadn't hit him hard enough because he grabbed my ankle from his spot on the floor, pulling me down to the ground with him. I tripped, catching myself quickly, trying to kick him off me with my other foot.

He might be a softer sort of man, but he was fucking strong and pinned both my legs down, dragging me towards him. I screamed out in rage, trying to hit him with fists and nails. Once I was close enough, he used his body to pin me down and forced my hands above my head. His lips found mine as soon as he had me restrained and I bit at his lip until I could taste the coppery taste of blood on my tongue. I managed to get a hand free and raked my nails down his face, using every bit of fight I had in me.

He wasn't having any of it. A growl of warning left his chest as he pulled off of me long enough to flip me and pin my hands back over my head. On my stomach, I had no fucking leverage, and I found him hard as he ground into my ass. I tried to buck him off as he pulled my pants down again. I was fucking fucked. There was no way to use his weight against him, and from this position, his larger frame could easily overpower me.

With no warning or preparation, he slid himself into my pussy. A pained gasp left my lips as he thrust into me repeatedly. He used one hand to hold down my wrists and moved the other under me, where he stimulated my clit. The fucking bastard wasn't going to just take from me. He was going to make me enjoy it. A moan slipped past my lips as he hit me in all the right spots. My core tensed as my orgasm built. Fuck, fuck, fuck!

"Enjoy it, *principessa.* Your body loves the feel of me. I can feel that sweet pussy tightening around me. You're so fucking wet and tight like this." He whispered in my ear, never losing his pace as I came apart at the seams.

A scream ripped from my lungs, a mix of torment and pleasure. "That's it. Come for me. Soak me in your sweet nectar, *principessa*."

I felt like I'd lost whatever fight was in me. My orgasm and fight leaving my body at the same moment. I hated myself at this moment as Lorenzo fucked me. Bringing me pleasure and my own special brand of pain. My nails dug into the hardwood floor as he continued to thrust into me.

If I couldn't stop things like this from happening, I might as well learn to end things as quickly as possible. Using what renewed strength I had, I pushed back. Meeting his thrust with my own. While my mind was screaming at me that this was wrong, my body wasn't on the same page. I'd enjoy what I could and do my best to take down Lorenzo's empire from the inside. I imagined all the ways I'd enjoy killing him. Moans left my lips as he stretched me, filling me. His own groans of pleasure filled my ears. If only he knew that my moans were over the scenes I played in my head where I tortured him, fileted him like a fish, and bathed in his blood while he begged for mercy.

CHAPTER FIFTEEN

Angel

Things were so fucking weird. Once Lorenzo was finished with me, he turned back into that charming persona he wore. He took his time to care for me and clean me of our combined fluids. Looking him over as he did, he looks so disheveled. His pristine hair fell out of place over his right eye and a small trail of blood trailed down his chin where I'd bitten his lip. Deep scratches marred his face where I'd been able to dig my nails into his skin. I took pride in the fact that he wasn't walking away from this incident without a scratch.

Once he was satisfied that I was clean, he insisted on carrying me back to my room, where he drew a bath in the oversized tube filled with lavender-scented bubbles and proceeded to wash my hair. I had no fight left in me at this point other than the burning desire to make him pay before this was all over. He was kind and caring as he washed me, which just fucked with me more. When he was finished washing my hair and body, he surprised me by undressing and getting into the tube behind me. Before I could protest, he pulled me back into him, fitted between his muscular thighs. I could feel him hardening again against my back as he pinned me to his chest.

"I'm aware this isn't what you wanted, but I want to make you happy." He said into my hair.

"You want to own me." I was seething.

"*Sì*, I want to own you. I want you to belong to me and only me. However, I want you to enjoy your time with me as well. Do me the honor of at least trying to be open-minded about your situation. I can take care of you and give you everything you could ever want in this life."

I didn't justify his statement with a response. I couldn't bring myself to. The chains binding me to this man just kept getting tighter. The more I fought, the tighter they'd become. In 28 days, Damon would be here or I'd be dead.

"Let me please you, *principessa*," he whispered, trailing kisses over my neck and shoulder.

It was time to get out of my own head and play this how it needed to be played. Emotions were getting thrown out the window and I would do what I needed to do. I leaned back into his touch, a light moan slipping from my lips.

I felt him smile against my skin as his hand found its way between my legs. I opened them wider for him as his fingers ran down my slit. In my head, I could imagine it was Damon's fingers instead. The thought had me moaning loudly in pleasure as he slipped two fingers into my warm center. His skilled fingers worked me ever closer to the edge. Before long, I was rocking my hips into his hand. He whispered praises in Italian against my skin as he moved his fingers faster, curving them to hit that soft flesh inside of me that had me screaming out my release.

CHAPTER SIXTEEN

Angel

Two weeks had passed and every morning I awoke to tangle in the sheets of Enzo's bed. He'd been insistent that I move into his room. The room itself was 3 times bigger than the one he'd had Cherry and me in. It was decorated in black and grey with accents of gold throughout. He had 'my belongings' moved into his walk-in closet, which was bigger than my old apartment, and the bathroom housed an oversized jacuzzi and a waterfall shower.

Slipping out of the bed, I made my way into the bathroom to shower and get myself ready for the day. I'd been spending the past few weeks snooping as Enzo allowed me more freedom to explore the grounds. Taking note of the guard shifts and where they were stationed around the grounds in the surrounding wooded areas. I needed to get as much information to the guys if they were going to succeed in taking over Enzo's business. I hadn't been able to send what I'd found yet, but I was making sure to keep an accurate mental note of everything they may need.

When I wasn't snooping, I was requested to accompany Enzo in his office or room, where he took his time in bringing me to orgasm. Every time he touched me, I had to imagine it was Damon instead and scrub myself raw in the shower until I felt halfway clean again. A part of me had to admit he was skilled in how he used my body, but it just didn't feel right. It hadn't been the first time I'd used my body like this. As if my sexuality were my own personal weapon, but it was the first time I had feelings for a man while sleeping with someone else. It was just wrong on so many levels. This is why I tried to stay as far from other people as possible. Caring about someone led to nothing but trouble and heartache.

After showering and getting dressed in a red sundress and black flats, I made my way down the hall to do some more exploring. Before I could really get anywhere though, a throat cleared behind me. Turning, I found Dante heading my way. What the hell could Enzo's bitch want now?

"*Il Capo,* would like to see you." He said before leading me to the office I'd become very acquainted with over the past few weeks.

I didn't say anything as I followed him. I'd learned really fast that opening my big mouth only had it being gagged or filled. I wasn't interested in having Enzo force his dick down my throat again. It took days to get the taste of him off my tongue.

I walked into the office ahead of Dante and Enzo waved his hand to dismiss him. He really was a little fucking bitch. He did whatever Enzo told him to do. Without looking back as the door was shut behind me, I walked over and sat on the edge of the desk next to where Enzo was typing away on his computer.

"You wanted to see me, Enzo?" I asked, running my fingers lightly over his exposed forearm. Play the part, Angel. That's all you have to do, I reminded myself.

He glanced at me over the rim of his glasses before taking them off to lay on the desk, "*Sì*, you have been on your best behavior these past few weeks so I wanted to take you out of the house for a little while."

I smiled at him, my fingers stopping their light track on his arm. "What did you have in mind?"

He flashed me that charming smile, showing off his pearly white teeth, "It's a surprise."

Surprise probably wasn't the best choice of word. This view was the most beautiful thing I'd ever seen. Enzo had wrapped up his work for the day and then drove us out to the docks where a large yacht awaited us. Now that I thought about it, I was sure we were only a few miles away from where Doc had put that tracker in my neck. The throat had me rubbing at the spot where he'd stabbed me and I could just feel the device underneath the skin embedded in the muscle underneath. I shook my head to rid myself of my thoughts as I made my way onto the boat with Enzo leading the way. The thing was completely decked out with lights and romantic Italian music playing over the sound system, and the crew set sail out into the open ocean.

There was nothing for miles as we continued to sail across the sea. The sunset on the water was breathtaking, and I simply sat at the front of the ship watching as the sky turned into golden colors. It was peaceful and I couldn't help that my mind continued to wander to Damon. What was he doing right now? Was he watching the sunset now too? I'd become a love-sick teenager when it came to him. A part of me still revolted at the idea, but if I wasn't going to be around much longer, the least I could do was stop lying to myself. Even if I did lie to everyone else.

"Questo tramonto non è nemmeno paragonabile alla tua bellezza, principessa."

I jumped, spinning around to see Enzo walking up to me. He was dressed casually in a pair of nice khaki pants and a button-up white dress shirt that had the top three buttons undone and his sleeves rolled up. He was attractive, but something was lacking. I couldn't ever imagine myself feeling for him like I did for Damon.

I rolled my eyes, turning back to look at the view. "Will you continue to talk to me like that when I have no clue what you're saying?"

He sat down behind me and pulled me into his embrace, watching the sunset with me. "This sunset does not even compare to your beauty, princess."

He whispered the words against my skin as his lips trailed along my exposed neck where I'd thrown it in a messy bun earlier in the evening. I leaned back into his touch while my stomach did flips, and not in a good way.

"I'm never going to figure out what you're saying," I said as his lips trailed down to my shoulder.

"You will learn, *principessa.*"

"I've been trying for weeks and still don't understand any of it." I huffed and shrugged him off my shoulder.

He simply chuckled and pulled me back into his chest. "We will discuss it further later. For now, let's enjoy our time together." He trailed his hands down my sides, to the front of my sundress, lifting the hem up my thighs slowly, "Would you care to dance with me, *principessa*?"

"I don't dance." My body felt tense, like my skin was too tight over my body. A suffocating feeling washed over me at Enzo's touch. Why couldn't this shit be simple? I just had to go and catch fucking feelings for someone. Fucking stupid.

Enzo stood, taking my hand to pull me up with him. The man was charming and graceful. I would give him that. He took his time leading me to the center of the deck, where there was plenty of space to dance. He spun me like I'd imagine someone spinning a ballerina before pulling me flush against his chest, one hand holding mine and the other delicately placed on my waist, "You've never had the right partner."

The dance was slow and sensual, going along perfectly with the soft music playing from the speakers that ran the length of the boat. I just followed his lead as he spun and turned me. I wasn't used to giving this much control to someone else. Even with Damon, there had been a sense that I had a say. With Enzo, it was all how he wanted things to be. He was at the wheel and I was simply along for the ride. Could I find comfort in my new situation for however long it would last? It was doubtful. Some way, somehow, one of us would end up six feet under.

CHAPTER SEVENTEEN

Damon

The crowd roared as my fist met my opponent's face, bone cracking beneath my knuckles on impact, and blood flew from his mouth. He fell to the floor, KOed, as the "ref" did the whole counting thing before lifting my hand in the hair while the audience cheered. Money was passed around, the smell of blood, sweat, alcohol, and smoke filling the air of the warehouse we were in.

These weren't legal fights, so the crowd was a mix of bigwigs looking to gamble away their fortune and scum alike. I ripped the tape from my hands as I left the loud cheers and blaring music for the silence of the empty locker room. The smells were worse here as I worked to rip the lock from my locker and take a swig from my water bottle. I needed a fucking drink.

This had been what I'd done every night while I counted down the days to either get the call that Angel was back or for me to storm that fucking place and get her out. I was hoping she'd make it out on her own, but it had been weeks. I'd heard nothing about her from Dimitri or Jensen. Last they knew, she was perfectly fine and still locked away in Lorenzo's mansion. She'd gotten the drive installed and now Jensen had access to everything. Dimitri was working on getting the big things handled and looking into replacing Lorenzo with someone in our pocket. We couldn't leave things to chance again. It was better to be a part of the business, no matter how much we hated it, but Dimitri was positive he could find someone to take the seat who would do as we said. No more stealing girls. No more forcing people into these situations. It would only be those who were interested in offering their services with well-planned out contracts that benefited everyone involved.

The sounds of music and cheers rang through the room as the door to the locker room was pushed open and in sauntered a pretty blonde in a suggestive outfit and heels. She smiled at me as she walked over, getting into my space. It took everything in me not to knock her skinny ass to the ground.

"What?" I snapped. I wasn't interested in what she had to offer or in wasting my time.

"Hey there, handsome. I was hoping you'd like to hang out tonight." She smiled, dragging her long-ass manicured nails down my bare chest.

"Not interested." My voice was clipped as I backed up a step, reaching into my locker to grab a t-shirt and tossing it on. If the bitch touched me again, I didn't trust myself to not start swinging.

The blonde seemed surprised that she'd been turned down. She tried to reach for my arm, but I was much faster, wrapping my fist around her slender arm and twisting until she whimpers in pain. Fear flashed in her big brown eyes, but I didn't care as my anger burned through me.

"Get out," I growled between my teeth, pushing her away from me. I didn't even have the energy to care as she scurried from the locker room.

Without a word to anyone else, I threw my crap in my bag and headed out, jumping on the back of my bike and heading back to Angel's apartment for the night. I'd been staying there since she'd been taken. The place still smelled like her lavender and lilac scent, and it was the only place that gave me a sense of calm while everything else was going to shit. My life was in chaos with Angel here. The worry was eating me alive while all I could do was sit here and wait.

I showered, throwing my wet hair up into a bun, and lay in the bed. Images of Angel during our moments together flashed through my mind as I lay in the darkness of her apartment. My hand found its way around my cock, working the length as I hardened at the thought of her. Heard her sounds of pleasure in my head. I imagined she was riding me right now, her head thrown back in ecstasy as her cunt strangled my cock. It didn't take me long to come all over my stomach, groaning her name as I found my release.

Soon. I'd have her back soon.

CHAPTER EIGHTEEN

Angel

We had spent the past five days on the boat.

Exploring small island areas off the coast and taking

a swim whenever we were anchored, and the sun was

too hot on deck. I found myself forgetting my worries

as the days passed and I was floating in the soft

waves. Almost forgetting what my purpose had been

for all of this. I wasn't Angel or a captive in a pretty

prison for a moment.

The weather had been perfect. Warm with a

slight ocean breeze and not a dark cloud in sight. The

evenings were cooler, which made the evening dinner

on deck perfect. The crew handled all the heavy

lifting and a private chef prepared all of our meals.

This left me with all the time in the world to pretend

this was the type of life I'd always wanted. I'd forced

myself into a sense of denial about my situation. Choosing to live in fantasy for as long as possible.

Enzo groaned from his spot between my legs. His tongue gliding over my clit in the aftermath of another orgasm that left me breathless. I moaned out his name, my fingers tangled in his hair. He'd made sure to let me know I was to moan out his name. The thought had me wanting to roll my eyes, but it was better to just get it over with instead of arguing about it. We'd been spending so much time in this bed that I'd lost track of everything he'd done with me. I'd found myself enjoying his touch more and more over the past couple of days. My body craved the release he offered and the haze of an orgasm. It was just another way to get out of my head for a bit. Afterward, I still felt dirty, wishing I was with Damon again.

His lips trailed to my inner thigh, which I knew held the scar of Damon's brand, "I wish you'd have this covered up, *principessa.*"

I propped myself up enough to look at him, plastering a teasing smile on my face. "Why do you have to ruin the moment like that?"

He crawled up my body, forcing me to lie back down as he positioned himself over top of me. I could feel his hard cock pressing against my entrance as I opened my legs wider for him. His lips found mine in a passionate kiss, our tongues colliding in a show of dominance. It wasn't filled with need and hunger like my kisses had been with Damon. I missed *that* sort of passion, but this could work. At least the sex was enjoyable, I guess.

It didn't take Enzo long to slide into my slick entrance. My walls clenched around his length as he thrust into me at a leisurely pace. His movement was precise as he continually hit that sweet spot. He enjoyed drawing out my release.

"Please, Enzo," I thrust my hips, needing more than he was giving me. I craved a rough fucking, but that wasn't his style. Sex was a dance, and he enjoyed getting me to that edge just to deny me. Where Damon tortured me with orgasms, Enzo denied me. Forcing me into a needy mess before he'd give me what my body needed.

His lips trailed down my jaw and throat, down to my breast, where he took one into his mouth. Sucking and biting at my hardened nipple. I moaned out his name as a plea. Begging for release. My nails dug into his back as he pushed me further toward the edge of blinding pleasure. All that could be heard in this small cabin were the sounds of skin hitting skin and my moans of pleasure as he slowly worked me up. He'd get me right there and then change his movements just enough to piss me off.

I grew tired of his games, using my strength to flip us over so that I was on top. Lifting myself and upping the pace. I fucked him hard and rough. Just the way I liked and needed it. Trying my best to pretend as if it were Damon's cock I was bouncing on.

His hands found my hips, his head tilted back as he groaned out in pleasure. Curses in Italian flew from his lips as I forced us both over the edge. My orgasm barreled into me so quickly my vision blurred and I lost myself in the bliss. His cock pumped up into my tightening cunt as he chased his own release. My name tumbled from his lips as he filled me. I collapsed on the bed next to him, trying to catch my breath. Our combined orgasms coated my thighs and a slight ache was apparent at my core.

In the moments afterward, I really hated myself. I hated that I enjoyed fucking Enzo. Hated myself because I had wished it had been Damon's come sliding down my legs as I made my way to the private bath where I'd shower away the evidence of what had just occurred. I couldn't stand to look at myself in the mirror anymore. I barely recognized myself anymore.

What the hell had I become over the past 22 days? Just 9 more days and this would all be over.

CHAPTER NINETEEN

Angel

Six Days left. That was all the time between now and when Damon would come.

Following the trip out on the yacht, we returned to Enzo's in a blissful sort of mood. He'd informed me that he'd be hosting another event in three days, similar to the one he'd taken me to prior. He told me things would be a bit different this time around, but he'd give me the details later.

I was happy to remain blissfully unaware of what there was to expect at another one of these events he liked to have. Hoping that I wouldn't have to see Damon at this one. I wasn't interested in him seeing me as this shell of a person I once was. One that bent to the will of her capture and didn't put up a fight. I couldn't stand to look at myself in the mirror most days because the disaster that looked back wasn't Angel anymore.

The days prior to Enzo's event were a blur of tangled limbs, searching around for any other useful information, and lots of scotch. Scotch was the only way I found to cope, and it reminded me of the taste of Damon. He had scorched his mark on my body and soul. He hadn't just branded me; he owned me. I was royally fucked.

Today was the big day. A group of women came in to see that I was prepared for the event to Enzo's specifications. They took their time getting my body washed and then slathered in creams and oils. They tried different hairstyles and makeup looks to make sure everything was perfect while I sat silently in a silk robe, nursing a crystal tumbler of scotch. If I had to go to another one of these fuckfest events there was no way I was doing it sober. I was really surprised however when they didn't dress me in a gown. Instead, they left me in nothing but a black lace thong, my black silk robe, and a pair of red bottom stilettos. This didn't bode well for me, but I was just drunk enough not to care.

When they were finished, they'd settled on my hair being left down in long waves, a simple smokey eye, and a bold red lip. If I made it out of this, I would never wear this color lipstick again. As they were finishing cleaning up their supplies, the doors opened and in walked the man of the hour.

He was dressed in black slacks with a baby blue dress shirt. The sleeve rolled up, as usual, to show off his muscular forearms and tattoos. I'd realized soon enough that he didn't have nearly as much ink as me. His tattoos were small and scattered across his arms. Outside of that was simple bare skin. Not once had I had the desire to trace the art with my tongue. It wasn't even remotely as enticing as the ink that covered Damon from neck to toe.

I really needed to stop thinking about him so much.

The women scurried out of the room with their supplies as Enzo walked up to me, taking a strand of hair between his fingers as if admiring the soft ringlets. "You look stunning, *principessa.*"

"Thank you, Enzo." As I drank from my glass, I smiled at him over the rim. I was already slightly drunk and my words sounded slurred, even to my own ears. I must have had more than I thought.

Enzo wore a look of annoyance as he took the tumbler from my hands and sat it out of my reach. "I need you to be on your best behavior tonight. You have an important part to play tonight for our guests, so don't be sloppy."

"You still haven't told me what my role will be." I glared up at him. He really pissed me off when he wasn't making me come.

"You'll be the main attraction tonight. A treasure to be seen and unable to be touched. I want every man and woman in attendance tonight to crave you." His fingers trailed along my jaw until he held my chin in his hands. This had been his power move with me since the beginning, and I had to fight the urge to snap my teeth at his fingers. "You're mine and I intend to make that known to everyone this evening. My own personal toy to do with as I please."

His words sent my blood boiling. I didn't have a say in any of this, but it explained the lack of clothing. He intended me to be a show like the other people he sold at these events. He wanted to use me to gain more profit. The hornier he could get the crowd, the more money they would be willing to spend on the others that they *could* get. I nearly rolled my eyes.

He didn't explain much more as he led me downstairs to the same doors as before. The sound of music and voices flowing into the hallway. I was glad that I'd drank enough to be slightly out of it. Though it made walking in these ridiculous shoes a bit harder. I had to grip tightly to Enzo's arm to keep from falling. Enzo released his hold on me and I stumbled slightly. He gave me a cutting look, which had my spine straightening as he stood in front of me. From his pocket, he pulled out what looked like a collar attached to a chain.

What in the actual fuck was that for?

He slipped the strap of black leather around my neck, fastening it quickly as I stared at him wide-eyed. He couldn't be fucking serious. Taking the chain in his hand, he yanked me towards him, forcing our bodies as close as they could be. "You will be my obedient little pet tonight, *pincipessa.* Just behave and put on a good show for all of our guests."

He loosened his grip on the chain, allowing me the space to back up a step. "Now slip out of that robe for me."

I hesitated a moment before pulling the string that held my robe together. The silk fabric glided over my skin as it fell to the floor around my feet. I set my shoulders back, trying to maintain some sort of dignity. At least that's what I told myself.

"Good girl, now open that pretty mouth."

This time there was no point in hesitating. I opened my mouth as he gripped my face while pulling a ball gag from his pocket. I guessed he didn't want me mouthing off in front of his *friends* tonight. He slipped the ball into my mouth and fastened it behind my head. He looked at me as if in praise for following his orders as he stood back to look me over.

"*Così bella.* Now on all fours. I want them to watch you crawl."

I did as he instructed. Sliding onto my hands and knees as he nodded for the guards to open the doors. He pulled on the chain, leading me into the room full of people in pretty gowns and expensive suits. I watched the floor as I crawled after him. If there is a god, please don't let Damon be here to witness this. If he saw me crawling like this, I'd set this whole fucking building in flames with myself locked inside the inferno.

He led me through the crowd, towards the front of the room, up a short set of stairs that lead to a raised stage area. Looking up through my lashes, I saw a bench that had an area for arms, legs, and a head to go. I had to assume it was a sex bench, because why wouldn't it be? He led me over to it, where he pulled on my leash, ordering me to stand.

I tried my best not to look at the faces of the gathering crowd as he moved me to take a place on the bench. The leather of the bench was cold to my skin as he strapped me to the thing, forcing me to have my ass in the air for all to see. I still wore the lacy thong, so that was a plus for now, I guess. My neck, wrists, and ankles were all restrained in leather belts as my hair fell down around my face, almost hiding me from the view of the crowd.

Enzo began speaking, but I couldn't hear a thing that was said. My heart was hammering in my ears, so I closed my eyes tightly with my head resting on the cushioned headrest of the bench. It wasn't long before I felt Enzo's hands on my hips.

"Be a good girl, *principessa*." He said, ripping the flimsy lace from my body, exposing my pussy and breasts to the crowd.

As if I had a fucking choice. He took his time running his hands over my ass before walking away for only a moment. What felt like soft leather replaced his hands. If I had to guess, it was a riding crop you'd see used at horse races. Enzo trailed the crop down my spine, down to my ass where he began to whip me with it. I tensed as the blows landed on my ass, whimpers leaving my open mouth from the sting. From this angle, I could already feel saliva running over my lips and chin. This shit was humiliating and my dumb ass was just taking it.

This time, the crop didn't land on my ass like I'd been expecting. It connected with my pussy. A moan fell from my lips as my fists clenched, pulling against my restraints. I was going to kill him.

This *punishment* continued for what felt like hours, but I was sure it was only a few minutes. Once the lashing stopped, I heard a belt being undone before Enzo slammed his cock into my throbbing center. I couldn't even enjoy it as he pounded away at me. Making a show of his prowess. I was sore from the crop and I was positive at this point that the nerves in my pussy had been numbed from the lashing. This wasn't meant to be pleasurable like my other times with him. Why did men think that pounding into a wet hole somehow made them more of a man? To me, it just seemed pointless and showed that they didn't know how to please a woman.

Enzo groaned as I felt him fill me with his come. The evidence leaked down my thighs onto the bench beneath me as he pulled out. A cheer rang through the crowd as I listened to him refasten his pants and belt.

"I hope you all enjoyed this little demonstration, as she will be open to paying participants for the evening, for your pleasure. I will advise that you steer clear of her mouth. This one has a bit of a bite. *Gustare*!" Enzo chuckled, giving my ass a final smack as he descended the stairs into the crowd.

What the fuck did he just say? I lifted my head, watching as he was patted on the back and handed checks from men in the crowd. This fucker had just sold me like a fucking piece of meat. I pulled on the restraints, trying to loosen them so I could get the fuck out of here. Scanning the crowd, my eyes landed on the face of Dimitri. A panic washed over me as I looked around to see if Damon was next to him. Thankfully, it seemed as if Dimitri had come alone. I was sure it had to do with their contract that he had to attend this fucking thing. I almost sighed in relief, knowing that Damon wasn't here to witness my *fall from grace.* Dimitri excused himself at that moment, slipping from the room and pulling his phone from his pocket as the door shut behind him.

The first man to ascend those fucking steps was a bald, muscular man. He looked like a bodybuilder in a fucking suit. As he made his way over to me, he tossed his suit jacket onto the table that housed all sorts of whips and toys. He ignored them all as he walked behind me and a nearly deafening sound of his pants and belt hitting the floor filled my ears. He grabbed my hair roughly, pulling my head back as much as he could with the restraint around my neck as he slammed into me. Tears stung my eyes as he fucked me with no remorse. His grip on my hair tightened as groans of pleasure came from him until he was exploding inside of me.

This treatment continued. Men took turns filling my pussy and ass for their own pleasure as my tears and saliva ran down my face. Come leaking from me, creating a mess on the bench. My knees slid on the wet leather, and the only thing holding me in place were the belts that wrapped around my neck and limbs. No one cared to clean me up after they were done. I lost count of the men after fifteen. They just kept lining up like I was some sort of fucking prize.

At some point, I must have blacked out. I blinked my tearful eyes to see the room empty and Enzo leaning in front of me, where he removed the ball gag and unfastened my restraints. Everything hurt and my limbs felt heavy. All I could do was watch him numbly as he removed me from the bench, cleaned me up with a damp rag, and carried my limp body up to the room we'd been sharing.

The last thing I remembered before my world turned black was him lightly tracing my shoulder and back with his fingertips.

"You did so well tonight, *principessa.*"

I awoke to the sound of Enzo talking in a hushed tone. Opening my puffy eyes, I saw it was still dark in the room and Enzo was standing by the open window, talking on the phone. He hadn't noticed I'd woken up, so I simply pretended to sleep and listened to his conversation. It was a mix of English and Italian, but I understood enough to gather what the conversation was about.

Jensen must have gotten my messages because from the sounds of things, Enzo's organization was crumbling. I could hear the anxiety and anger in his voice as he told whoever was on the other end of the line to get things fixed.

"Gabriele, get this mess cleaned up... I don't give a shit if it's impossible. Figure it out, *imbecille.*" Enzo hung up the call before sliding back into the bed behind me.

He wrapped his arm around me, pulling me back closer to his front.

Two more days and this crap would be over.

CHAPTER TWENTY

Damon

"It's almost time to go in and get her. She's been sending Jensen information on and off for the past month on top of him being able to hack the systems. She even gave us detailed time stamps of shift changes for the guards in and around the estate. We have everything we need to take down his operations, and I've sent teams out to take care of anyone who may try to step in. We've contacted the man who we are appointing in Lorenzo's place and he's on our side." Dimitri said while looking around the dingy locker room.

"Is she still alive?" I asked, unwrapping my bloodied hands.

Since I'd walked out of Hellfire almost a month ago, I'd been spending all my time fighting in underground fight rings. I'd made a good amount of profit from the matches I'd been winning, and the violence was something I needed to keep from storming into Lorenzo's place to get my girl back. I was wound tight, just waiting to hear something. Any sign that she was okay or that she needed me. I knew she didn't need me to save her, but this waiting was killing me.

"Her last message was sent two days ago. Now, can we leave this filthy place already? I'm going to have to burn this suit." Dimitri sounded absolutely disgusted. He'd always been a pompous ass and a neat freak. I did notice pity washed over his face for a moment when he mentioned hearing from Angel a few days ago. He was hiding something, but I wasn't in the mood to push.

"Yeah, let me just grab my shit. It's time to go get my girl."

Everything was in place as we parked down the road from Lorenzo's estate. A group of men had been sent out to get rid of the guards so that we could make our way in without anyone being able to warn their boss. I didn't need that fucker making his way out with my girl. She would be mine again before the sun came up in the next few hours.

My fists clenched in anticipation as I sat there with my men, waiting for the green light. It felt like I'd been sitting here for days when it had only been about ten minutes. I lit another cigarette, doing anything to keep myself busy. What was taking those idiots so fucking long? Sitting in this SUV, I was going to start popping off my own men if they didn't hurry the fuck up.

"All clear, sir." One of my men said over the comms.

"You heard the fucker move out." I nearly yelled at the driver.

He didn't take offense as he put the car in drive and drove us through the gates of the estate. My men stood there ready to open the gate as we drove through. Once we were through the gates we jumped out of the car and made our way up the long drive surrounded by its own little forest on foot. We used the trees and bush for cover as we made our way up to the front of the house. My personal explosives guy was already working to rig up the front entrance as I made my way over to a hiding place behind a large oak tree.

"Detonation, in ten seconds. 10, 9, 8, 7, 6, 5, 4, 3, 2..."

A loud explosion shook the ground as the door was blown off its hinges. Without wasting a second I rushed into the building. Shooting any of the guards who fired on us. My men followed me inside the foyer as we took out Lorenzo's men. It was the perfect image of destruction as dust and gunfire filled the air.

I almost rushed towards Angel as I saw her being led away from the action by Lorenzo and his right-hand man. She was dressed in a casual set of black leggings and a cropped top. From here, I could make out bruises across her body, despite her tattoos. I wanted to rip those clothes from her body and see just what damage that fucker had done to her. Her eyes snagged on mine before she turned to the man at her side. She made quick work of throwing a right hook and elbowing him in the gut. As soon as he doubled over, she grabbed his gun, firing a round into the guy before pointing it at Lorenzo.

CHAPTER TWENTY-ONE

Angel

Everything was in complete chaos tonight. Smoke and gunfire filled the air as Lorenzo and Dante led me through the front room. Lorenzo was shouting orders in Italian over his earpiece, not paying any attention to me. Stealing a glance at the front door, I could see Damon opening fire on anyone who stood in his way as he forced himself into the mansion. His eyes met mine, and a fire engulfed me from that simple look.

I glanced away long enough to see an extra gun inside of Dante's holster and I knew exactly what I'd need to do. As fast as I could, I rounded on the man, throwing my fist into his chin in an uppercut, elbowing him in the stomach, and grabbing the gun before he knew what had hit him. Just as fast, I unleashed bullets into him as his body crumpled to the floor and a puddle of blood began to form under him on the grey floor. Fuck, I'd forgotten how good it felt to be in control of someone's life like this. I quickly took out any of the guards within range as Lorenzo turned to face me with wide eyes.

I wasted no time at all pointing the gun at him. "Tell your men to stand down."

The shock morphed into anger as he did as I'd instructed. There were few men left standing as the foyer had turned into a war zone. Damon's men quickly took out the rest as they unarmed themselves, and all that was left was an eerie silence.

"Was this what you'd been planning all along, *principessa*?" He asked as he glared at me.

"Not exactly. I didn't plan on living this long," I said as I walked closer to him.

"*Avrei dovuto sapere che sarebbe successo quando eri così facile da controllare.*"

"You know, I always hated when you'd talk to me like that," I said, tilting my head to the side.

Lorenzo simply smiled as Damon made his way over to stand at my side. His men went off to search the rest of the grounds for any loose ends. Lorenzo still stood as confident as ever. I didn't understand what he had to be confident about. He'd just lost, but he just smiled that charming smile of his. I didn't like this. Something was wrong and I could feel it in my gut.

"Are you alright, Angel?" Damon asked, taking the gun from my hands.

"What took you so fucking long?" I glared at him as he pointed his gun at Lorenzo's head. His lips turned up in that crooked smirk that I had missed these past weeks. He was covered in blood and damn if it didn't do something for me.

"I wouldn't celebrate so quickly. Things just got interesting." Lorenzo's smile turned wicked right before a gunshot was heard from behind us.

Pain ripped through my back and chest as I fell towards the floor. Fuck. I glanced around as my vision began to blur around the edges to see Dante with a gun pointed at me.

"I tried to warn you, *principessa,*" Lorenzo said, as he pulled a gun from his back and pointed it at Damon.

It was getting harder to breathe, and I could feel the blood dripping from the corner of my mouth. The metallic taste filled my mouth as I coughed up more of my own blood. I didn't even think as I pulled a dagger from Damon's leg holster and launched it at Dante. It hit him square in the arm, causing him to drop the gun he'd been pointing at Damon. The last thing I heard was gunfire as my world faded to black.

CHAPTER TWENTY-TWO

Damon

My heart stopped as I watched my girl fall to the floor, a steady puddle of blood forming around her body from the bullet wound. How she managed to throw that knife to disarm Lorenzo I had no clue, but I needed to act fast.

As swiftly as I could, I aimed my gun at the dying man on the floor, shooting him in the head. He slumped to the floor, finally dead, as I rounded on Lorenzo. A quick death was far too nice of an ending. I wanted him to suffer, especially if anything happened to Angel. A blind rage overtook me as I thought about Angel and I launched towards the fucker, tackling him to the ground as my fists met his face. He tried to fight back, but it was a useless battle. All I could see was the blood and hear the sounds of bones cracking. My knuckles ached, but I couldn't stop even as the man beneath me stilled. The rage had taken over as my fists connected one after the other.

I wasn't sure how long I spent beating him. It could have been minutes or hours. I didn't stop until hands wrapped around me, hauling me off that piece of shits body as I fought to punch his face through the fucking floor. Things didn't come into focus again until my brother stood before me and slowly his and Zack's voices filtered in through the blinding fog that had taken over.

"That's enough, brother. Let's focus on getting Angel out of here. She'd lost a lot of blood and isn't looking good. We have to get her to the doctor." Dimitri said, holding me in a steel gaze.

Looking over, I found Zack and a medic looking over Angel. Her pale skin was ghostly white as they hooked her up to all sorts of machines to check her vitals. Without asking for permission, I walked over, scooping her into my arms to rush us out to the waiting van.

"If he's not dead, detain him for me. I want him fucking alive." I spat, rushing out the door to get my girl to the doctor. Fuck, she just had to be okay.

CHAPTER TWENTY-THREE

Angel

Everything hurt. My head felt like someone had split my head open with an ax. It even hurt to breathe as I blinked my eyes open to the white-washed ceiling, where ugly fluorescent lights shone brightly. Who turned the fucking lights on so damn bright and where the hell was I?

Trying to sit up, an intense pain shot through me, stealing the breath from my lungs as I fell back onto the uncomfortable as fuck bed I was in. My mind was drawing a blank of what was going on and I was pissed that even the slightest movement had me in so much pain.

"Glad you see you awake, baby girl."

That voice. I'd know that voice anywhere. My eyes cut to the side to see Damon leaning against the door frame, a bouquet of red roses in his hand as he smirked at me. My face must have shown my surprise as he prowled into the room, filling the small space with his muscular frame.

Flashes of him storming Lorenzo's place flashed in my mind, the sound of the gun going off before I fell to the floor. I winced as the memories replayed in my mind. My mouth was dry and scratchy as I tried to speak. My tongue felt like sandpaper and as if my tongue filled my mouth, leaving me unable to make a sound.

Setting the roses on the bedside table, Damon reached for a cup of water, bringing the straw to my lips to drink, "Slow, Angel. You've been out for a few weeks."

Once I'd had enough water to unstick my tongue from the roof of my mouth, I looked up at him, glaring. "I hope you weren't worried about me."

I still ached as I fought the pain to sit up. Like hell if I was going to be stuck in this fucking bed. I groaned in pain as I took in my body. My chest was wrapped in gauze and a hospital gown of some sort hung around my waist loosely. As if they hadn't wanted to cover up the bandages in case they needed to get to them.

"I was terrified I'd lost you." Damon whispered as he sat on the edge of the bed, which dipped under his weight.

I scoffed, rolling my eyes. Just because we admitted we cared for each other didn't mean we had to do all that lovey dovey shit. That just wasn't who I was. "It'll take more than a fucking bullet to take me out."

Damon smirked, the gesture not reaching his eyes. For someone so big, he was a fucking softie sometimes. Worry laced his brow as he took my hand in his, kissing the knuckles. In doing so, I saw his knuckles wrapped in bandages, taking in the cuts that marred his perfectly tattooed skin. He looked like he'd been through hell and hadn't been sleeping, if the dark circles under his blue eyes were any indication.

"What happened to Enzo?" I asked, just above a whisper. I hoped he was dead.

For the first time, a true grin graced his kissable lips, "I'll show you once you get out of here."

I didn't like the answer, but didn't have the energy to fight him. With a sign, I laid back down, giving my body the time to recover. How long would it take for this shit to heal and why was it so painful to breathe?

"What exactly happened to me?" I asked, not daring to look at the man sitting next to me as I stared blankly at the ceiling.

"That bullet went through your lung. You were nearly dead once I got you to Doc. He worked hours to keep you alive. For five days, you were on machines that breathed for you before you started breathing on your own again." His deep voice was rough like gravel as he recounted what had happened after I was shot. Purposely skipping over anything about what had happened to Enzo.

No wonder I felt like shit, and it was just about to get worse.

"Damon, I need Doc to run some tests for me." I avoided his gaze as I pulled my hand from his.

"What happened, Angel?" His voice was so calm. Goosebumps broke out along my arms. That was the voice of a man out for blood. But that blood belonged to me.

CHAPTER TWENTY-FOUR

Damon

It took everything in me to stay seated as Angel recounted the things that were done to her the night she was sold, as if she were nothing but a fucking sex toy. I wasn't sure how I managed not to go on a rampage once Angel had fallen asleep.

My little Angel. So battered, and yet she didn't let that bring her down. There was no regret or remorse on her face. No shame in what she'd been through. Only a deep rage that burned in her cold steel eyes. How could someone remain as strong as she did with all she'd been through in her life? She was a force that was strengthened by all the disaster that followed her throughout her life and she continued to fight. Thriving in her darkest moments.

Using everything done to her as a way to harden her own armor.

When I was sure she would be sleeping the rest of the night, I left the room. A calm washing over me as I made my way into the hall. I needed to make a phone call. My girl would get her revenge and I'd revel in watching her burn the world to the ground as she collected the blood she was owed.

Stepping outside, I lit a cigarette, letting the smoke burn my throat and lungs as I made some phone calls. I'd find out every single person who placed their filthy hands on my girl. They'd regret ever being born when she was finished with them.

CHAPTER TWENTY-FIVE

Angel

They made me stay in the fucking hospital for another week, running a shit ton of tests, and having me speak with a counselor before they would discharge me. All the tests came back clean despite how many fuckers had stuck their filthy dicks in me during that "party". I tried not to think too much about all that.

It had been interesting talking to the quack, at least. She must have been new, because when she looked over my file, she seemed to admit about me seeing a therapist regularly. I'd made it clear it wasn't going to happen. I'm sure that took some strings being pulled by the boys, but I didn't care. Only one thing was going to make me feel better. Letting the blood of those fuckers paint my skin to hear their screams of pain. I wasn't sure how I'd find them, but I wouldn't stop until every single one of them died at my hands.

I still had a long road of recovery, so I had plenty of time to make the necessary plans. Until then, Damon and Cherry fussed over me. Cherry was a sniveling mess when Damon dropped me off at my old apartment to rest. The little group from Hellfire was there to welcome me back, including that pretty redhead who'd been on display at the first event I'd gone to with Enzo. I'd been thankful when Damon ushered everyone out for me to rest.

After two weeks of being taken care of, I was over it. Throwing on a pair of sweatpants and a tank top, I left the apartment while Damon was showering. It felt good to feel the wind against my face as I drove through the city on my bike. I'd left my phone and a note on the bedside table, so Damon wouldn't burn down the entire city, hopefully. I was already expecting a lecture, so I stayed out until well into the night.

By the time I made it back, I was ready to collapse in my bed again. Pulling up, I was surprised to see an array of nice vehicles in the parking lot. That couldn't be a good sign. Everyone was in my apartment when I walked through the door.

Cherry launched herself at me, wrapping her arms around me in a tight embrace that left pain shooting through my chest.

"Oh my god, Angel! We were so worried about you! Where were you? Are you okay?"

Prying myself from her grip, dragging in a lungful of air that left me wincing as I made my way to the counter to pour myself a shot of whiskey. I was hurting after my day out and I needed something to numb that feeling. One wasn't going to be enough, so

I threw back 2 more before I looked at the group of people in the small space. If they were all going to keep coming around, I'd need a bigger place than this shitty studio apartment.

"Everyone out." Damon said in a deathly calm voice, never taking his eyes off me.

Cherry was about to protest until Dimitri placed a hand on her lower back to lead her out the door. Zack following close behind. If they were all here, who the hell was working at Hellfire, anyway? Looking between the bottle and shot glass, I decided maybe it was useless to dirty the glass. Tipping back the bottle before I made my way to the bed, reclining against the headboard to relax. The air was tense as Damon watched my every move. A calm before the storm settling over us. I took another swig before cutting a glare in his direction.

"I left the note, so there was no reason to cause a scene. I was fine."

Anger flashed in his eyes as he stalked towards me, his large hands gripping the railing on either side of me as he towered over me. If he was trying to intimidate me, he'd have to do better than that.

"Shut the fuck up, Angel." A growl sounded deep in his chest, sending a wave of heat to my core. All I could do was smirk, taking another drink from my bottle.

"I'm fine." I seethed through my teeth.

His hand lashed out, gripping my chin as we glared at each other. "You will stay in this bed until you are completely healed. I'm not going to risk losing you because of your stupid ideas."

"You don't fucking own me, Damon." Anger filtered into my voice, sounding like a hiss.

Damon's fingers dug into my skin as his lips crashed against mine. He engulfed me in his heat as our mouths battled for dominance. A clash of tongue and teeth as his hand moved down to my throat, the other tangling in my hair as he consumed me. The way this man tried to dominate me made my blood boil. Anger and lust mixing in a toxic combination, leaving me breathless and hungry.

I wasn't sure how it happened, but Damon's mouth traveled down my body, biting in places, leaving a maddening ache in my core as my pants were ripped from my body. His hands were roaming, but never touching where I needed as I gasped for air. Catching my breath was still a challenge, but I couldn't bring myself to stop him as he delved between my thighs. His tongue flicked that bundle of nerves until I was moaning out his name. My fingers tangled in his long hair as I chased my own release. I was so close already, my pleasure building as he slammed his fingers into my core, sucking my clit into his mouth in the perfect rhythm.

"Oh god," I moaned, nearly choking on the lack of air filling my damaged lungs.

He didn't stop until I was coming on his tongue and finger. A silent screaming left me as my body tensed. Fuck. What the hell did this man do to me?

He lapped at me as I came down from the high, wincing as the air filled my lungs again. He watched my every move as his tongue traced the mark he'd left on my inner thigh. A challenge gleaming in his eyes.

As soon as I could breathe again, I pushed a foot against his chest, forcing him away from me as I got up and locked myself in the bathroom. I was starting to think that fighting with him was a losing battle.

CHAPTER TWENTY-SIX

Angel was finally getting back to normal after her eight weeks of recovery. She'd been hell to deal with. Not wanting to stay in bed to actually rest. A few times I'd even resorted to cuffing her to the bed. The only thing that kept her sated was promising her pleasure.

Just the thought had me aching to fuck her, but she wasn't ready for that yet. I'd been counting down the days until I could sink balls deep into her warm cunt. Waiting for Doc to give me the okay. Today was that day, but I had plans for her first.

My girl was currently in the shower, getting ready to go out today. I'd told her I had plans for us, but she didn't know exactly what my little surprise was. I lounged on the sofa, flipping my knife in my hand as I waited for her to walk out the bathroom door.

The water cut off and after a few moments; she was strutting out that door in a pair of low-rise, skin-tight jeans, a black crop top, and her leather jacket. Her hair was a wet mess around her beautiful face and it took everything in me not to take her right here and now. My cock straining against the zipper of my jeans.

"Well, let's go." She rolled her eyes, heading straight for the door, and I followed close behind her. Steering her towards my bike as we walked outside.

"Is this necessary? I have my own." She asked, crossing her arms over her chest with a glare in her eyes.

Ignoring her comment, I threw my leg over, handed her a helmet, and started the bike. The rumble of the engine vibrating through me. "Get your fine ass on this bike. Now, Angel."

She huffed, but did as she was told, climbing on the bike behind me. As soon as her arms wrapped around my waist, I took off. Heading towards Hellfire.

CHAPTER TWENTY-SEVEN

Angel

He still wouldn't tell me what the hell we were doing at Hellfire as he led me through the dark main floor. His hand wrapped tightly around mine as he led me towards the back and down the stairs to the basement. Who the hell did he have down here this time?

The place was silent as he unlocked the door to one of the rooms, flicking on the overhead fluorescent lights. I couldn't see shit until he stepped from in front of me, showing the view of a very familiar man dangling from chains attached to the ceiling.

My eyes widened in shock as I took in the shape of the one and only Enzo. He was out cold, but breathing. His face and body were a bloody mess. No longer looking to be the powerful man he'd been before all this. He was at the mercy of someone else now.

Damon moved, tossing a bucket of water on the battered man before me. "Wakey, wakey."

He taunted as Enzo came too with a jerk; the chains rattling with the movement. He seemed surprised when his eyes landed on me standing in the door. I could have sworn I saw fear wash across his face for a moment and I felt a wicked smile grace my lips.

"I've been working on getting names for you, Angel." Damon spoke, stepping in my line of vision, his hands lightly grazing over my arms as I looked up into his deep blue eyes. "This is your fight. All their lives are yours to take. So I've saved this asshole for you and collected the names of the others."

I felt tears burn the backs of my eyes. He wouldn't take this from me. Keeping Enzo alive for me to deal with and collecting the names of the men who'd been forced on me. He'd just handed me the best gift anyone ever had. My heart swelled, and a smile graced my lips.

"Him we save for last. Let's get to work."

I took my time going through the list. Taking out each person who'd taken part in the shit show at Enzo's estate. Taking my time to humiliate and ruin each person's life before ultimately disposing of them. In total, there had been thirteen of them. I didn't know how many had been involved. My mind clouded the event in an effort to protect me from the things they'd done to me while I was chained down like a rabid animal. Blocking out all that shit had probably helped me from spiraling, that's for sure. Now I could relish the feeling of holding their lives in my hand. Damon never interfered in any of it. He got me the names and information I needed while I took care of the rest.

Now there was just one more person left.

Enzo hung from the chains still in the basement. Covered in blood and his own filth. Given just enough to stay alive until I was ready for him.

Tonight would be his last on this earth, and I wanted

to savor every moment of it.

Hellfire was closed, and I locked the doors

behind Lily and Cherry as they left for the night.

Damon sat at the bar, a tumbler of his favorite scotch

in his hand as he watched me. I hadn't told him what

my plans were, but he knew tonight was the night.

Tossing my things onto the counter next to him, I

made my way down to the basement, Damon

following closely behind me.

CHAPTER TWENTY-EIGHT

Damon

My dick was hard as I followed Angel down to the basement. My eyes focused on the sway of her hips as she walked into the room where Lorenzo was being held. I loved watching her work, taking out every shred of anger on the men who'd hurt her. Fuck. She was beautiful in her element.

The door to the room swung open, Enzo hanging from his chains and the smell of filth and decay filling the air. He didn't deserve any comfort after the shit he did to my girl. Selling her off to anyone willing to pay him. If this weren't Angel's kill, I'd make him suffer.

I closed the door behind us, taking a seat in the metal chair next to it, straddling the frame and leaning forward on the backrest as I watched my girl look over an array of toys lain out for the night. I hadn't been sure what she wanted to do, so I added a little of everything on the counter.

Enzo was silent, watching her with fear shining in his eyes as she ran her hands over the knives and weapons in front of her. Her hand eventually wrapped around the hilt of a boning knife. A wicked smile spreading across her pale rosy lips. She hadn't been wearing her normal red lipstick since coming back. I found it best not to ask her about it, even though I missed the color.

"Damon, care to go get me some salt and lemons from upstairs, please?" She asked without looking at me.

I stood, going upstairs as she took the knife in her hand, shredding the clothes from Lorenzo. I would gladly bow at her feet if she'd asked me to. The confidence she normally wore bleeding out of her and she started working on the flesh of one of Lorenzo's thighs. His screams filled the air until the basement door shut behind me.

I rushed to the bar, grabbing the things she'd asked for before going back down. The man's leg was in tatters. The flesh hanging from his thigh in odd places, other pieces littering the plastic on the floor beneath him. Curses in a mix of Italian and English spilled from Lorenzo's mouth as he jerked against the chains holding him suspended in the air.

"Hold still. I wouldn't want you to bleed out before I've had my fun." Her voice came out through gritted teeth as she fileted the man like a fish. It reminded me to never get on her bad side, though the thought of being at the mercy of her blade made my cock ache as it pressed against the zipper on my jeans.

Content to simply watch, I sat the lemon wedges and bowl of salt on the counter next to her before taking my seat again. Resting my chin on my forearm as I watched to strip the flesh from muscle and bone until he was nearly skinned alive. The sight was gruesome, but seeing Angel covered in blood made me feel savage. The glee in her eyes shining as the fucker screamed and begged for mercy as she worked.

"How are you keeping him awake?" I asked as she stood back to admire her handy work.

"Gave him some amphetamines before this." She said simply, tilting her head to the side as if in thought.

She flipped the blade in her hand once before stepping over to him again, taking his chin in her other hand as her thumb ran along his bottom lip. "You have such a beautiful mouth, Enzo."

A sly smile spread across her lips. Enzo's eyes widened in shock as she brought the blade to the corners of his lips, slashing it across his cheeks in a permanent smile. He yelled out in pain as blood dripped down his chin to his chest, thrashing against the restraints as she walked over to the counter, tossing the knife onto the countertop, and poured a handful of salt and lemon juice into her palm.

I smirked as she walked back over, taking his damaged face into her hand, forcing the mixture into his fresh wounds. The sounds of gagging pain filling the air once more.

"Oh, shut up. You know, it wasn't so hard to get all the information on your business and find someone else to take over in your place. Someone who would follow our orders on how things would work from now on. Gabriele was happy to be of assistance." Enzo was glaring daggers at her now as her fingers pressed into the bloody gashes along his face. "Everything you worked for crumbling to the ground and being taken over by the people you hate most. It's too bad you'll never get to see it."

She pulled a blade I hadn't noticed from her back pocket, using it to saw his flaccid penis from his body before shoving it down his throat. He gagged, thrashing once again as he choked. Struggling to breathe as she held his mouth closed with her hand, nails digging into the bloody flesh until he became still. Only 53 seconds and he'd died from asphyxiation.

She backed up from his body, shedding the bloody clothes she wore before turning to face me. Blood covered her pale flesh, her tattoos and the blood standing out as her shoulders relaxed. Sauntered over to me, she slid her hands into my hair, which I'd left down tonight, as she brought her lips to mine. Kissing me with a new sort of hunger. Slipping my hand around her throat, I stood, pulling her where I wanted her as my tongue explored her mouth. Hot and needy as our tongues fought for dominance. Pressing her back against the door, I moved my hands to her thighs, lifting her so that I could grind my jean covered cock against her soaking folds. God, I could feel the heat through the thick material, feel the wet spot forming against me.

"Take out my cock," I ordered, trailing my mouth along her jaw, down her throat. The taste of her sweat and blood filling my mouth as she reached to undo my pants.

As soon as my cock was free, I slammed into her waiting cunt, groaning out in pleasure as her warm heat surrounded me. I wasn't soft or loving at that moment. I fucked her ruthlessly until she was screaming. Her head hitting the door with every thrust of my hips as she held onto me. Nails and her heels digging into my back until she was coming on my cock.

"Mine," I growled into her ear, causing her pussy to spasm around my length.

"Shut up and keep fucking me."

Her order was breathless, and she didn't have

to tell me twice.

CHAPTER TWENTY-NINE

Angel

I was so fucking tired. I'd lost count of how many times Damon had fucked me once I'd finished off Enzo. First in the same room as Enzo's body hung there rotting, then on the floor, in the shower, in the car, in this very bed we lay in once we'd made it back to my apartment.

Now I was wrapped in his arms, a tangle of limbs as we lay there trying to catch our breath while I rested my head on his broad chest. Groaning when he sat up, moving me from my comfortable spot. I just wanted to rest so I could ride his cock. I was insatiable and wanted more of him. Things had been off for too long since getting better. This was actually the first time we'd actually had sex since everything went down. Other than him eating me like his last meal, we hadn't been doing anything else.

Damon moved from the bed and I watched that fine tatted ass as he walked over to his pants by the couch. My core clenched in want as I watched him move to pull something from the pocket, tossing the jeans back onto the floor before walking back over to the bed. My eyes snagged on his hard dick as he stood at the foot of the bed. I still couldn't see what he had in his hand as he used the other to pull my leg until I was on my back, legs spread wide as he climbed between them, taking a place there as he placed an open box on my belly. I stared wide-eyed at the ruby red ring that starred up from the little jewelry box, gasping when he flicked my clit with his tongue.

"Damon, what the fuck is this?" I asked, trying to sit up.

His large hands gripped my hips to hold me down to the bed. "Marry me."

It wasn't a question as his tongue slipped into me, fucking me at a fast pace as my hands tangled in his hair.

"Fuck," I moaned out, my thoughts about the ring shattering as he lapped at my core, sucking my aching clit into his mouth.

For a moment, I forgot what he'd just said as my world shattered and I came on his tongue. Damon wasn't done with me yet as he reached to move the box from my stomach before flipping me over onto my hands and knees, slipping easily into me from behind. His hand found its way into my hair, yanking my head back as he pounded into me.

"Answer me, Angel." He growled. Enunciating every word with a hard thrust.

"Yes." I couldn't form any other words as he plowed into me, another orgasm building in my core. Fuck. What had I just said?

EPILOGUE

"I can't believe you actually said yes!" Cherry squealed as she gushed over the ruby that now graced my ring finger. It was a silver band, wrapped in diamonds, with a large ruby stone in the center glistening under the lights of the bar.

"Don't remind me." I used my right hand to take another shot as we sat at the bar of Hellfire. Cherry still hadn't let go of my hand as she looked over my new engagement ring. Even I couldn't believe that I'd said yes when Damon asked.

I'd admitted my feelings for the asshole and I'd stuck around after healing from my gunshot wound. Yeah, that shit hadn't been fun. It was hard to believe everything that had happened. The gunshot wound, the recovery, taking out all those men, and finally getting to end things last night with Enzo. It felt like a weight had been lifted. Like I could finally have a life.

"Need another shot, Angel?" Lily asked from behind the bar.

She'd been the pretty redhead from the first party Enzo had taken me to. Zack had outright bought her that night to get her out of there. She hadn't had a place to go, so she stuck around. She was a sweet girl, and she'd been a big help with things at Hellfire. Zack was wrapped around her finger, and it was nice to see him so happy.

"Please," I handed her my empty glass as Cherry finally released my hand.

"Don't let her get too drunk. She still has work tonight." Damon said from behind me.

"On second thought, I'll just take the bottle." I reached over the counter and snatched up the bottle of scotch before turning to face my soon-to-be husband. I wasn't sure I'd ever get used to that.

He was smirking at me, a fire in his eyes as he looked over my body. I took the stopper out of the bottle and tipped it back. Chugging a good bit of it before hopping up from my stool.

"Yeah, about that boss, not happening. I'm calling out sick." I made my way up the stairs to the VIP lounge, knowing that Damon wasn't far behind me.

Walking in, I plopped down on the soft sofa and took another swig from the bottle, watching Damon walk in and shut the door behind him. He almost prowled towards me. A hunger in his eyes, as if he were stalking his prey. I just smiled at him and offered him the bottle once he was standing in front of me.

Taking the bottle from my hands, he placed it on the coffee table and pinned me to the sofa. His hand wrapped around my throat as he forced me to lie back, making himself comfortable between my legs.

"What am I going to do with you, my little Angel?" He growled, before capturing my lips with his in a tangle of tongue and teeth..

I kissed him back, slipping my hands into his long hair to pull him closer to me. Him mixed with the taste of scotch, was euphoric. I couldn't get enough of him, of his touch. I was his completely regardless of how much I tried to run from those feelings. And he was just as much mine as I was his.

Angel Ashford. It had a nice ring to it.

The End

Or is it…

ACKNOWLEDGEMENT

I still find it completely insane that this is my third book and that there is more to come! None of this would have happened without the support of my writing buddy Brittany, my friends, family, TikTok fam, and most of all you, my amazing readers who keep giving my books a chance.

Without you and your support I couldn't do the thing I love most. For the majority of my life I've felt as if I've been floundering with no directions. Then one day Brittany demanded I write a book about a random idea I had. Now, for the first time in my life I think I'm finally on the right path. I've found something I'm passionate about that brings me joy. As Britt likes to say, she created a monster.

I love writing and I hope you will continue to join me on this crazy ride. There are more stories stuck in my head that I can't wait to share and this isn't the end of Hellfire. I have far too many surprises up my sleeve to just end things.

ALSO BY HAYLEY BRIANA

COMING SOON

Hellfire: A Hellfire Novel
A Hellfire Novella 3
A Hellfire Novella 4
Fall From Grace
Fall to Sin
A Darkside Fairytale Book 1
A Darkside Fairytale Book 2

ABOUT THE AUTHOR

Hayley Briana is a small-town girl from North Carolina, currently residing in Colorado. As a stay-at-home mom & wife, she needs some major self-care in the form of a good cup of coffee (or wine) and a good book. Escaping into a world of fantasy is Hayley's favorite pass time outside her day-to-day responsibilities. When she's not adulting or writing you can most likely find her tucked away in her home library.

For more info on Hayley and what she is working on please visit HayleyBrianaWrites.com

Follow Hayley on Social

Instagram.com/hbrianawrites

TikTok.com/@beautyandthebookcase

www.ingramcontent.com/pod-product-compliance
Lightning Source LLC
Chambersburg PA
CBHW040901010826
48978CB00013BB/1108